TAKING A CHANCE

BY LINDSAY McKENNA

Blue Turtle Publishing

Praise for Lindsay McKenna

"A treasure of a book ... highly recommended reading that everyone will enjoy and learn from."

—Chief Michael Jaco, US Navy SEAL, retired, on Breaking Point

"Readers will root for this complex heroine, scarred both inside and out, and hope she finds peace with her steadfast and loving hero. Rife with realistic conflict and spiced with danger, this is a worthy page-turner."

—BookPage.com on Taking Fire
March 2015 Top Pick in Romance

". . . is fast-paced romantic suspense that renders a beautiful love story, start to finish. McKenna's writing is flawless, and her story line fully absorbing. More, please."

—Annalisa Pesek, Library Journal on Taking Fire

"Ms. McKenna masterfully blends the two different paces to convey a beautiful saga about love, trust, patience and having faith in each other."

—Fresh Fiction on Never Surrender

"Genuine and moving, this romantic story set in the complex world of military ops grabs at the heart."

—RT Book Reviews on Risk Taker

"McKenna does a beautiful job of illustrating difficult topics through the development of well-formed, sympathetic characters."

—Publisher's Weekly (starred review) on Wolf Haven
One of the Best Books of 2014, Publisher's Weekly

"McKenna delivers a story that is raw and heartfelt. The relationship between Kell and Leah is both passionate and tender. Kell is the hero every woman wants, and McKenna employs skill and empathy to craft a physically and emotionally abused character in Leah. Using tension and steady pacing, McKenna is adept at expressing growing, tender love in the midst of high stakes danger."

—RT Book Reviews on Taking Fire

"Her military background lends authenticity to this outstanding tale, and readers will fall in love with the upstanding hero and his fierce determination to save the woman he loves.

—Publishers Weekly (starred review) on Never Surrender
One of the Best Books of 2014, Publisher's Weekly

"Readers will find this addition to the Shadow Warriors series full of intensity and action-packed romance. There is great chemistry between the characters and tremendous realism, making Breaking Point a great read."

—RT Book Reviews

"This sequel to Risk Taker is an action-packed, compelling story, and the sizzling chemistry between Ethan and Sarah makes this a good read."

—RT Book Reviews on Degree of Risk

"McKenna elicits tears, laughter, fist-pumping triumph, and most all, a desire for the next tale in this powerful series."

—Publishers Weekly (starred review) on Running Fire

"McKenna's military experience shines through in this moving tale . . . McKenna (High Country Rebel) skillfully takes readers on an emotional journey into modern warfare and two people's hearts."

—Publisher's Weekly on Down Range

"Lindsay McKenna has proven that she knows what she's doing when it comes to these military action/romance books."

—Terry Lynn, Amazon on Zone of Fire.

"At no time do you want to put your book down and come back to it later! Last Chance is a well written, fast paced, short (remember that) story that will please any military romance reader!"

—LBDDiaries, Amazon on Last Chance.

Available from
Lindsay McKenna

Blue Turtle Publishing

DELOS

Harlequin/HQN/Harlequin Romantic Suspense

SHADOW WARRIORS
Danger Close
Down Range
Risk Taker
Degree of Risk
Breaking Point
Never Surrender
Zone of Fire
Taking Fire
On Fire
Running Fire

THE WYOMING SERIES
Shadows From The Past
Deadly Identity
Deadly Silence
The Last Cowboy
The Wrangler
The Defender
The Loner
High Country Rebel
Wolf Haven
Night Hawk
Out Rider

WIND RIVER VALLEY SERIES, Kensington
2016
Wind River Wrangler
Wind River Rancher

2017
Wind River Cowboy
Wrangler's Challenge

Taking A Chance

Dedication

To my many global readers: You're the greatest! Thank you for reading my stories and I hope it gives you a 'time out' from this chaotic world of ours for at least a few hours!

CHAPTER 1

Mid-October
Tucson, AZ

ALI FELT ANXIOUS and frustrated while trying
to project an aura of calm for her younger
sister, Cara. At age twenty-six, two years younger
than herself, Cara shakily stood between their
parents, trying to smile, but it was forced and
brittle. She tried to look "normal," but that word
would never apply to her again.

Ali watched as her parents, their arms around
her sister's waist, carefully walked down the steps
from the Operations building. Her sister was still
weak after having been a prisoner in Mexico for
more than two, long weeks.

The family was now at Davis-Monthan Air
Force Base in Tucson, Arizona. Above them, two
A-10 Warthogs thundered overhead. Ali had
helped rescue her sister, along with an Artemis

Security team. Afterward, the group had flown from Mexico to Tucson for a long, arduous debriefing with the FBI, CIA, DEA, and ATF. Everyone was exhausted, but Cara looked pale and weak. Ali suspected her sister would head straight for bed as soon as she got home.

Cara was a kindergarten teacher for Delos Charities, and had been kidnapped off a street in Tucson less than a month ago while walking the five blocks from the school to the home where she and her parents lived. She had been stuffed into a car trunk, tied up, duct-taped across her mouth and drugged. She was then driven into the Sierra Madre Mountains of Mexico in the state of Sonora, which butted up against the US border. There, she was thrown in with three, female German tourists, also abducted by Azarola's men. The four women were kept imprisoned in a mountain fortress belonging to the drug lord, who planned to sell his captives to sex traffickers in Southeast Asia.

Cara found out that a container ship anchored at Puerto Nuevo on Baja's west coast would be leaving shortly for Asia. She would be hidden in a truck and driven dockside, put on board the container vessel, and join over a hundred other kidnapped women from North and South America, as well as children as young as eight, already promised to buyers. Fortunately, their plan was foiled by Ali and the Artemis

Security team.

Ram Torres, Ali's black-ops partner on the rescue mission, came and stood quietly by her side. They traded brief looks with one another. Ram's presence always calmed Ali as nothing else ever could. She could feel tension radiating off him, his green eyes narrowed upon Cara as the family slowly approached them. Ram and Ali had been working together for two years in the military and she was highly sensitized to his feelings. Right now, he was feeling very protective of Ali, knowing that her sister would be leaning heavily upon her in the coming weeks after being rescued.

Cara's forced smile made Ali's stomach clench. They had always had very different personalities, even as children. Cara had always wanted to be a teacher, and had gloried in her job teaching kindergarten. All she'd wanted was to make a positive change in the lives of under-privileged children. Ali, on the other hand, had gone into the Marine Corps at age eighteen.

"Ali!" Cara said brightly, "Thank you for coming!" Her parents released their arms around her, allowing her to move freely toward her sister.

Swept up in her grief for her traumatized sister, Ali forced her own wooden smile, opened her arms, and took Cara into her embrace. As her arms wrapped around Cara, Ali could feel her sister trembling, and Cara clung tighter and tighter to her, burying her face against Ali's shoulder.

As they separated, Ali saw the worry in her parents' eyes. They knew Cara had been shattered by the experience—who wouldn't be? And afterward, she'd been debriefed, trying to answer questions along with the German women who had also been rescued. Authorities had asked them detailed questions about Azarola and his fortress in the mountains, where they had been kept prisoners.

Ali knew that each woman had undergone a thorough medical exam by a female doctor on base, and then spent hours with an Air Force psychiatrist. All that debrief material would be sent to Artemis Security, the in-house security firm for Delos Charities. The top-secret debrief would also be sent to other security and law-enforcement agencies worldwide who were dealing with this situation.

Ali was itching to read that report! As she released Cara, she saw that her skin was stretched tight across her high cheekbones, her black hair drawn into a pony tail, her dark-brown eyes almost black with terror etched deep within them.

Ali knew her baby sister did not have the internal grit that she did. Cara had always been the "soft" one in the family, as her father, Diego, had once confided to her. Mary, her mother, once told her that Cara needed protection from time to time.

"Cara, I'd like you to meet Ram Torres, the man who led the Artemis team to free you and the others," Ali said.

Cara turned to the tall, dark-haired man with intense green eyes. "Thank you, Mr. Torres." She stuck her hand out toward him, her voice trembling, "I remember you from that night you came to rescue us. Thank you . . . "

Ram managed a gentle smile, knowing that his hard, weathered face had been known to frighten women and children. He gently grasped Cara's damp, cool hand. "You're welcome, Señorita Montero."

"Call me Cara," she insisted, releasing his hand. She glanced at her parents, who stood nearby, and asked wearily, "Mama? Papa? Can we go home now?"

"Of course, *cariña,* dear," Mary said, coming forward, sliding her arm around Cara's waist again. "Papa put our pick-up in the parking lot across the street. Come this way."

Hesitating, Cara gave Ali and Ram an anxious look. "You're coming with us, aren't you? I don't feel safe alone. I was told in the debriefing that Mr. Torres would be staying with us at our home for a while to help me feel safe. Is that right?"

"Yes, ma'am," Ram said, speaking up. "I'm your personal security detail. Your parents have given me their guest bedroom and I'll be in the house and accompany you wherever you go. You'll be safe, Cara."

Ali saw her sister's face mirror utter relief hearing Ram's words of reassurance. She knew he could project quiet strength to her sister and her parents. He was a wonderful anchor for someone to hold onto.

Ram had been right in his raw assessment of Cara's state: she was traumatized to the point of being lost, unable to grapple with what had happened to her. Actually, Ali still wasn't sure what had happened to Cara, and this made her even more eager to get her hands on the debrief report that Lockwood had.

"Oh," Cara whispered, giving Ram a grateful look, "that's wonderful. Thank you for doing this, Mr. Torres."

"Call me Ram, and it's my job—one I'm happy to provide, by the way. Just know that I'll be with you for as long as you need me." He gestured to Ali, who stood nearby. "And remember, your sister is a trained operator, just like me. You actually have two guard dogs in the house protecting you. Ali is just as good as I am at being a personal security detail."

Cara gave her a grateful look. "I-I know. But it's nice to have both of you so close. I-I worry that Azarola will send men back here to take me away again."

"That's not going to happen," Ali told her.

"A-are you also staying with us, Ali? Tell me you will, okay?" Cara begged.

"I'm staying, Cara." Ali reached out, briefly touching her sister's slumped shoulders. "You're safe now. And there's no way Azarola will come after you again. Ram and his team put a huge hole in their operations. They aren't focused on you any longer. They've got their hands full with other issues they have to address, okay?" She gave her sister a look of confidence, hoping it would reassure her.

There was no way Ali was going to appear weak, unsure, or hesitant around Cara. She knew what it took to make her sister feel stable again. She'd spent their formative years being her sister's protective shield, so it was easy to move into that role once more for Cara's sake. Instantly, she saw her grow a little less frightened.

"That's wonderful!" Cara wobbled. She reached out, gripping Ali's hand. "I'm ready now. Let's go home."

RAM WATCHED THE family dynamic as the observer he was. Mary, the mother, was a Yaqui Indian. Diego, the father, was Mexican, and they'd had two beautiful daughters, Cara and Ali.

He remained a shadow in the background

while Diego drove their extended-cab truck back to their one-story, pink stucco home in southern Tucson, near the Pascua Yaqui reservation. Tucson was built upon the sprawling Sonoran Desert, dotted with saguaros and other types of cacti. Farther to the south, near the Mexican border, were rugged volcanic mountain ranges. The city boasted a large metropolis that was home to a healthy mix of Caucasians, Hispanics, and other ethnicities, drawn to the area by thriving business and a major university.

The family lived in a simple, but well-loved home. Every inch was well cared for. The six-foot adobe wall built around the home's one-acre lot matched the color of the desert. The pink stucco house sported a Spanish red-tile roof and a spacious yard, half of which featured a big garden out in the back. Palo Verde desert trees with their namesake green bark, provided shade from the hot sun overhead. The yard was well taken care of and showed pride of ownership.

Night-blooming cereus cacti were in each corner and Ram imagined the hand-sized white or pink blossoms were magnificent when they bloomed for one night of the year.

His heart was centered on Ali, however. He knew her well from years of working with her in their SEAL team in Afghanistan under Chief Wyatt Lockwood's leadership. They had worked well together on ops, even though they had tangled on a personal level.

He amended that thought. She knew he was walled up and unable to emotionally trust anyone, and hated not being able to connect with him, so they'd ended up sniping at one another, instead. At the time, she had wanted more from him than he could give her—or anyone else. She hadn't known that he'd barely survived a painful, lonely childhood.

Now, as Ram looked around, the simple beauty of the large, two-thousand-square-foot house struck him. As they entered the residence, he admired its airy, brightly lit, open quality. The windows were large beneath a cathedral style roof, and the rooms were light and bright.

He was also looking at it through the eyes of an operator. Where were the possible places an enemy could penetrate, in case he needed to get Cara out of the house and to safety?

He hung back, watching Mary take her younger daughter down a red-tiled hall to her bedroom on the right. Ali had followed and Diego had gone into the kitchen to make everyone coffee. Ram thought about his own upbringing—his father was a pimp who owned a broken-down, old hotel in Nogales, Mexico, and his mother was a white prostitute with a drug addiction. They had come together and produced Ram, then settled into the hotel his father used as a brothel. Ram had grown up there, and when he was old enough to realize his shameful family roots, he was so humiliated he never spoke of his so-called family to anyone. As Ram grew older, he discovered that his father had never married his mother. He was just a "mistake" that had happened one night.

Ali's family, however, was like a storybook version he'd always dreamed of having. Here, both daughters were wanted from the time they were born. The warmth between Diego and Mary was genuine—Ram had rarely seen genuine affection between men and women at the hotel where he'd grown up. Several of the prostitutes, however, took him under their wing when they saw his mother had no interest in Ram. Starved for affection themselves, they would hug, kiss, and make a fuss over him.

When he wasn't with his substitute moms, Ram was assigned a room to live in alone. He ate in the kitchen with Joshua and Sophia, their cooks, who spoiled him with little pieces of dessert they weren't supposed to give anyone but his father.

Ram pulled himself out of the past when he saw Ali come out of Cara's room, her face dark with worry. He remained in the living room, holding her gaze as she walked over to him. Reaching out, he touched her slumped shoulders.

"How are you doing?" he asked, observing that she was close to tears. Ali wasn't one to cry.

In fact, he'd never seen her cry in the years he'd worked with her. Despite his instinct to hug her, Ram forced himself to remove his hand from her shoulders. They had both agreed to try and start over with one another, to establish a new relationship—one that was aware of their old habit of sniping at one another, and replace it with more patience and understanding.

Wiping her eyes, she gave him an apologetic look. "She's not good. She's a mess, Ram, just like you said she'd be. I have this awful gut feeling that more happened to her than she's telling us. Mama's with her right now, holding her, because she's sobbing her heart out."

"Mary is the right person to be with her right now, Ali." Ram said. "Look, this is going to be really hard on all of you, every day, for a while. There'll be no let-up, no relief for any of you, and no safe place you can get away from it, either."

Ali lifted her chin, staring up at him. "You sound like you've seen this before, Ram."

He wasn't going there. Ram had never spoken of his past, his childhood, to anyone—ever. "Let's just say I've seen it happen before." He cupped his hand around her elbow, drawing her over to the lavender, velour couch, urging her to sit down with him. He left a foot of space between them as he sat next to her.

"My poor parents," she murmured, keeping her voice low. "I know they aren't equipped to handle something like this."

"Home is the best place for her, though." Ram said reassuringly. "It represents safety to Cara. It's where she'll heal best." Just as the closet where he had made his bed and slept at night was his safe place in that hotel. It was small, dark, and enclosed and Ram felt protected in there. It was the only place where he felt that way while growing up. "Cara probably feels safer in her bedroom, doesn't she?"

"Yes, she does," Ali said, wiping her eyes again. "She's got a ton of stuffed animals in there. As a kid, at night, she'd love it when Mama tucked her in with her big, fuzzy bear. Cara loves that bear, even to this day. The poor thing is just about hairless, it's been held and loved so much over the years."

"She'll probably hole up in there for the next few weeks because it represents safety to her, so don't be surprised."

"God, Ram, I know I wouldn't react this way. I'd want to establish a fixed routine that I liked to anchor me. I wouldn't hide myself away."

He heard the pain and confusion in her voice. Again, he fought against reaching out and holding her close. Ram knew it would probably shock the hell out of her if he did that. Theirs had not been a warm, intimate relationship—just the opposite: it had been contentious, challenging, even angry and confrontational at times. He hoped that the kiss they had shared on the op to rescue Cara and the German women, was creating more trusting opportunities for them to heal their past—and get on with a future he wanted with her. It seemed like a far off vision and something he was sure probably would not ever come true—but he had to try. And he had to try and pace himself with Ali because of all the stress on her right now. He could see how she was scrambling to deal with her sister's psychological state and support her bewildered, anxious parents—ignoring her own suffering in the meantime.

Ram silently promised her that he'd be there for her. Ali had no one. Now, they had a fragile, tentative relationship budding between them. Until then, they had been out of touch for three years.

"Ali, you have a lot of inner strength. Sure, you've seen the underside of life in your job, but you've got survivor genes in your blood. When you went through something challenging you rose to the occasion and became stronger. Cara is different. She's just the opposite of you." He tried to give her a look he hoped was sympathetic. Ram wasn't good at revealing his true emotions, but he knew Ali needed some gentleness right now.

"You're right about that, Ram. Every time something challenged me, I took it head on and I got stronger because of it."

She sat there, resting her elbows on her knees, hands clasped between them, frowning. "Mama and Papa are not helicopter parents, Ram. They never were. It's just..." her voice fell to a helpless tone, "Cara *never* had a shell, never showed any strength, and I have no explanation for it."

"Not everyone is born strong when they enter this world of ours, Ali. She's one of those who didn't. I think your parents did the best they could to strengthen her and help her stand on her own two feet. She did go to college here in Tucson, she got a degree, and she's out working in the world. That shows she's got the basic skills to survive. Before this, she didn't hide in her home, avoid getting a job, and just live off your parents. In her own way, she did the best she could."

Morosely, Ali whispered, "Yes. I guess I want her to have my internal strength to deal with this trauma, and I just don't feel it in her."

"She'll gather it at her own speed and time," Ram counseled. "I know when you get knocked down like this it takes time to get back up."

Ali gave him a quizzical look. "How do YOU know all of this?"

Ram could see how much anguish she carried in her for her sister. "Because I was raised in a hell no one wants to be dropped into," he admitted heavily. "In a sense, I know what Cara is going through. I know what it takes to pull yourself up by the bootstraps when no one is there for you. At least Cara has the three of you, and you have no idea how much support that is giving her right now. You're feeding her strength and continuity to grab at the hands you're holding out to her. Just give her time, Ali. Give her space. Be there when she wants you, let her cry in your arms, and let her talk it out. But it's going to be on her timetable, not yours. That's what your challenge is." He held her tear-filled gaze. "You want her to get better faster because that way she won't have to suffer so much pain for such a long time. You all want to shorten her time, the duration of the pain she has to flail through and come out the other side of."

Sniffing, Ali studied him in the filling silence between them. "I know so little about you, Ram."

He heard the tremble in her voice, saw sympathy come to her eyes for him. Before the truce they'd had a few days ago, he'd have walled himself up to not feel anything close to sympathy for his personal struggle. Now, he tried to change it because he desperately wanted to be emotionally available for Ali in order to help her. If he walled up like he usually did, she'd feel rebuffed and he couldn't help her at all. Knowing that humans felt nurtured and safe when another human opened themselves up to them, he tried his best to do it for Ali, right now. She deserved help in this and Ram knew he could give it to her if he had the strength and the guts to do it.

He'd never done this for anyone—not even himself—he'd been a harsh taskmaster with himself in order to survive. Looking into her luminous golden eyes with a sheen of tears across them, watching her struggle not to cry for her sister, it became a little easier to remain vulnerable with her at this moment. "In time I hope to share more with you, Ali. But our focus has to be on Cara, being guides of a sort to her, to help her negotiate her trauma. We can't do it for her, but we can understand it and more important, feel where she's at, discover her pace on her healing journey she has to undertake."

He saw Ali lick her lower lip. It was something she did when she was grappling with something important. There was no question she fiercely loved her sister. His job, as he saw it, was to get Ali to understand the speed of how Cara was going to heal. And it wasn't going to be on Ali's timetable and that's what she had to grapple with first. He could see her thinking about his words, see her responding to him remaining open to her for the first time. There was confusion in her expression, trying to reset herself to him because this was a new path for them both.

She scrubbed her face with her hands. Lifting her chin, she met his placid gaze. "Thanks for sharing that with me. It helps me see Cara in a new light, a different one. You're right, Ram. We all heal at our own pace."

His mouth crooked more in a grimace. "Yeah, and it's not a smooth, straight road, either. It's full of twists, turns, and sometimes falling back on itself, and you feel like despite whatever steps forward that you made one day, you're back at square one again."

"I get that. I've seen it in myself." She rubbed her hands down the thighs of her jeans. "I need to reset myself to Cara's speed."

He gave her what he hoped was a tender look. "Yes. You're the right person to do this and I know you can. Your mother and father play different roles with Cara and they're going to struggle just as much as you are to understand their daughter's trauma."

She tilted her head, her voice low with so many feelings. "I never knew until just now how wise and good you are at assessing others, Ram. I wish . . . I wish I knew this side of you so long ago when we worked together."

He shook his head. "Wrong time and place, Ali. You can't do missions like ours and be touchy-feely about it. There's no place for emotions out on the battlefield."

She gave him an impatient look. "I'm talking about the times back at base. With the team— with me."

Surprised, Ram stared at her. "And how would that have changed anything?"

"I would have realized you had a soft, compassionate side, Ram. That you do understand human beings, that you are self-aware in ways I would never have guessed before today."

"I'm not like this often," he warned, giving her a wry look.

"But you are doing it for me. So now I'm seeing another side to you, Ram. And I like it—a lot. From now on, don't stop being like this with me. That's the side of you I really need right now. Could you do that for me?" she pleaded, searching his eyes.

Ram felt as if he'd been knocked sideways by an invisible sledgehammer. Ali had never pleaded or asked him for help on anything before. Her sincerity staggered him emotionally. He felt his heart opening up even more to her than before. Ali had a gentle side to her and she'd shown it often to the Afghan children in the villages. How he'd fantasized that she could someday offer that side of herself to him—and she was doing it right now. Bathed in the simple honesty of her feelings, Ram found himself absorbing them like a greedy, starving thief who had just found a pile of gold. Allowing her voice to whisper through the halls of his guarded heart, his mouth softened out of its normal, hard line.

"This is all new for me, Ali. I'm not good at

it. I'm trying, but it's harder than anything I've ever tackled in my life. You need to know that. I'm not perfect. You know that better than most. And I make mistakes, a lot of them." His voice grew weary. "And I'll make them with you as I try to be there to support you through this. Don't expect me to always have the right words, okay? I've just never allowed myself to do this—to open up to someone else before—I feel pretty raw and unsure about myself. I question if I'm doing it right or if I'm saying the right things to help you, not harm you."

Ali closed her eyes for a moment. When she opened them, she whispered unsteadily. "Because you care for me, Ram, you'll be imperfectly perfect for me. When you care for another person and you have their heart in your hands, you'll always try to help them. And no, it won't always be perfect, but you have to trust that I know that. I won't take the mistakes you make the wrong way. I'll know you're trying. That's what's really important here: you are trying. And Ram, for me that's enough. That's more than enough."

CHAPTER 2

Mid-October
Tucson, AZ

RAM COULD FEEL the tension in the Montero household, even at 0500 in the morning when he'd awakened. It had been two days since Cara had returned home, to her place of safety. He saw the stress on Diego's face, a gentle father who was trying to understand his daughter's sudden change in behavior. This was all new, these storms of weeping, screaming, and sudden fits of anger when Cara would lash out at those who loved her.

Ram sat in his bedroom across the hall from Ali's. He'd awakened and pulled on a black t-shirt, Levi's, and sneakers. Then, he'd thumbed through the debrief file regarding Cara. It had just arrived from Wyatt Lockwood at Artemis. His gut churned, knowing that Ali was going to read it, too, since Wyatt had also sent her a copy. He knew it was going to tear her apart. A lot more had happened to Cara than they'd first thought. *Dammit!*

He closed the document on his laptop, and glanced around at the room. Everything about it was cheery and bright, from the ornate, brightly painted red and yellow wooden chair from Mexico to the dawn light filling the window. The curtains were feminine, a white gauzy material with rainbow ribbons sewn together in a slender border. He wished with all his heart the beauty and warmth of this home could diminish the impact of the report awaiting the Montero family, but it couldn't.

He smelled bacon frying and figured Mary was probably up making breakfast for everyone. When he stood, he heard his stomach growl—it was part hunger, part stress. Taking a deep breath, he opened the door and quietly walked down the hall to the kitchen.

To his surprise, Ali was at the stove cooking, not Mary. Halting for a brief moment, absorbing her beauty, he saw that she had just washed her black hair. It fell halfway down her back, glinting with blue highlights. Her jeans enclosed her long, firm legs, and she wore a bright red t-shirt with capped sleeves that brought out the gold tones of her skin. He'd always found her beautiful, and a new ache settled in his chest, filled with longing and loneliness.

In the past two days, he'd seen the love that Mary held for Diego. It was inspiring for him to see a man and woman who truly loved one another. He watched how they comforted each other in so many small, yet important ways as they worked through Cara's trauma and her unpredictable moods. Ali had been raised with love, pure and simple—unlike him—and it was eye-opening for Ram to observe fondness between a married couple up close.

Mary and Diego were openly affectionate, always touching each other lovingly. A few times, Ram had entered the kitchen and saw Diego kiss Mary's cheek, his hand on her back, comforting her. Another time, Mary was outside weeding their large garden, and Diego came by, knelt down, and helped her. There they sat, on their hands and knees, laughing and smiling, love mirrored on their faces.

Ram had entered a new world, and he wanted this world for himself and Ali. Last night, he'd had a dream that he and Ali were on their hands and knees in the black, fertile soil of a new garden that was just sprouting. His heart sang every time she looked over the row of plants straight at him, her eyes filled with love for him and him alone. And her smile . . . *mi Dios*, her smile melted him until he was an emotional puddle. How he had felt in that dream remained strongly with him, embedded in his heart. He knew Ali's love was deep and strong; she had always been openly affectionate with their teammates, like a little sister with her big brothers. She would laugh and mercilessly tease and play jokes on the guys, but she was careful never to embarrass or humiliate them.

Except for Ram. He had put himself off limits to her in every possible way.

Now, he wanted just the opposite. He liked the feelings that wrapped around him every time he thought about his dream, with Ali's golden eyes shining with adoration for him. Her lips were so damned sexy and alluring, curved, and playful. The look in her eyes was wicked with burning heat and her need of him as her man.

Her man. Every aspect of the dream had been filled with hope and joy. But based on his life experience so far, dreams didn't come true. Look at how often he'd dreamed of getting out of that hell hole of a hotel and escaping the tawdry scum who fed upon one another inside it. As a child he couldn't put what he felt into words, probably because all he saw was ugly, selfish, cold, and heartless. To this day, he couldn't understand why any woman would become a prostitute. There was nothing good about it for the woman. And the johns? They were needy, selfish, abusive, narcissistic men who used and abused the women they had paid for. It sickened him as a child and later, as an adult.

Pulling out of his reverie, his gaze moved appreciatively down Ali's long spine, to those sweetly flared hips of hers, and those long, firm, curved thighs. She was perfect, he decided. But it had taken him twenty-nine years to appreciate Ali on this new, alluring level.

Two days ago, when they talked out on the couch, he'd seen his words affect her in a new, positive way. He'd seen a light of understanding enter her eyes when he'd shared a bit from his childhood. Ram hadn't meant to go there, but it was all he had, his whole world experience for eighteen years had been centered on that seedy hotel he called home.

Since his brief sharing, he'd felt better about himself, a sense of release. He even felt better about himself and Ali. It felt damn good to share something that would help her, instead of tearing her down. Now he wanted to build her up and show her how helpful he could be during this tough time. This new intimacy, while just in its beginning stages, was feeding both of them in a profound way. And it was just in time, because Cara's situation had created a black cloud hanging over this house, where it would live for some time to come.

For once, he could be a harbinger of healing words and actions that would nurture and support Ali.

"Hey, Ram . . . "

He snapped his head up, deep in thought. Ali was smiling at him over her shoulder.

"Are you hungry?"

"Yes." *For you.* Of course, those words never left his mouth. Instead, he ambled toward the counter near the stove where she was working. "That bacon sure smells good."

"Did I wake you up banging pots and pans around in here?"

"No, I was up already," he told her. He wasn't going to tell her about the debrief sitting on her laptop. Ram wanted this time alone with her. Maybe it was selfish, but he didn't care. To him, Ali was an oasis of calm, and she made him happy. "Is there anything I can do? Set the table?"

"Sure," she said. "You know where everything is. I got up early and was hungry."

"Yeah, everyone else is still asleep," he said, bringing down two plates and setting them next to the stove. "What got you up at the crack of dawn?"

"I don't know," she said, shaking her head. She took some bacon out of the skillet, placing it into a plastic basket lined with paper napkins. Draining off the grease, she pulled over the bowl of eggs she'd prepared earlier. "You're up early, too."

"I had a good dream," he admitted, putting

flatware on the table along with paper napkins.

"That's nice. At least someone gets them," she muttered, pouring the egg mixture into the skillet. She added shredded cheese, chopped white onions, and some sliced, mild green chilies to it.

Ram came over and watched her scramble the eggs with a whisk. "Are you having nightmares? Flashbacks?" He knew from personal experience that those with PTSD routinely had them, and with the stress in the household, Ali might be getting them again. Stress always brought them back for him.

"Yes," she growled, unhappily. "I should expect it. I don't know what all has happened to Cara, but she's having a bad time, losing sleep, having flashbacks . . . "

Ram wanted to come over and slide his arm around her hunched shoulders and offer some tenderness. She sounded deeply troubled, but said nothing more as she split up the scrambled eggs, dividing them evenly onto the plates. He walked over and picked up the plates.

"Come on, let's eat," he invited, careful not to sound bossy.

Placing the iron skillet aside, she said, "I'm not hungry anymore, but I know I have to eat."

Ram pulled out the chair for her and she halted, her brows flying up in surprise, looking at him.

He gave her a slight grin. "What? Are you going to tell me you never knew I was a gentleman?" He'd never have done this for her in the team. Amusement replaced the darkness on her face, and he saw that his teasing had a positive effect on her. That was another revelation for Ram.

"You took the words right out of my mouth, Torres," she chuckled, sitting down. He sat opposite her at the round table, formed from carefully placed staves of saguaro cacti that had been glued together. The grayish inner wood of the magnificent cactus had been filled with plastic, the surface smoothed and transparent, revealing the ribs and holes within it. The glass top had been placed over it, giving a person a look at the woody inner world of the world-famous cactus.

Ram had found out that one of Diego's side businesses was carpentry. The man was a talented artist, and he loved working in the large garage attached to the house. He sold handmade furniture to people all over the Southwest. Diego was making a name for himself, and the saguaro table was a prime example of his creativity at work. At some point, Ram intended to visit the garage to look at the furniture he was producing. Diego was an example of a simple man who was succeeding by focusing on nature's creative beauty for others. Ram absorbed the man's way of living, feeling inspired by it.

"Your mother looks pretty stressed out," Ram said between bites. "Is that true or am I off base?" He decided he was going to open up more. Instead of analyzing every word before speaking, he'd openly present them to Ali and see how she reacted.

Buttering her toast, she said, "Mama is very psychic. She feels a lot around Cara, but Cara isn't saying much. Right now, all she's doing is hiding in her room. She doesn't want to come out, holds her stuffed bear, and stares out the window. Mama's frustrated because she thinks something terrible happened to Cara, but she can't prove it."

Ram said nothing, knowing what was in that debrief she would read shortly. He wasn't going to stop her from doing it because it wasn't his place to do so. His job was to pick up the family's pieces after Ali read it.

"When a person feels those things," he said, "does knowing them make it worse for that person? Like being able to get inside someone's head to know their secrets, or in this case, to discover what really happened? Is that why it's more stressful for your mother?"

Ali gave him a pleased look. "I never realized the depth of you, Ram. That's exactly where Mama's at. I'm not as good as she is about 'feeling' people, but I sense tragedy and grief around Cara, things I've never felt around her before."

"You and your mother are very much alike," Ram agreed. "And I see your father's work ethic in you, as well. Who does Cara take after?"

"My grandmother Victoria, on my father's side, I think. His mother was very co-dependent, a fragile person, afraid of living life alone, and her husband was very protective of her. She best expressed herself through her paintings, which were very beautiful." Ali gestured toward the living room. "She did all the oil paintings you see in our home."

"Incredible," Ram said, impressed. "Maybe she had what we call an 'artist's temperament'?"

She laughed, "Could be. I, on the other hand, can't draw a circle! I missed out on the artistic gene from the family."

He grinned. "You can sure as hell shoot from a mile away and hit a target, though. Not many people in the world have that skill." He saw her grimace. "Hey, that was a compliment."

"I know . . . thanks." She looked up at him. "I guess I never took after my parents. Only after I went into the military did my skills come out."

"Yes, and you've saved a lot of lives, Ali. Never forget that."

Ali leveled a look at him, and gave him a look of praise. "I never thought I'd say this, Ram, but you're good for me. You show me the other side of the dark world we fight in. Sometimes, I think I'm losing my way."

He felt a deep sense of satisfaction within, a new sense of wonder that simply by opening up, he could feel almost euphoric. Especially when Ali responded so positively to his halting words of praise. Her appreciative response, the way she held his gaze, was like balm restoring his fractured soul.

Clearing his throat, he rasped, "I'm glad. I'm going to start reminding you of all the good things you do, Ali. How healing you are to others. You've always had a pure heart."

If Ram hadn't been watching her for a reaction, he'd have missed a look so exquisitely tender appear, it stole his breath away. The moment felt profound between them as they gazed at one another across the table. All the tension in Ali flowed out of her, revealing a woman who was terribly human, vulnerable, and needing his support, his healing words.

Ram had never realized the impact that positive words could have, and this new awareness made him boldly press on. Ali was sitting there before him, remaining fearlessly available to him, trusting him.

He'd missed so much. *So much.* But Ali was giving him a second chance. When she didn't have to defend herself against him, she could relax and open up to him. Another flood of emotion, this one rich with promise, brought back his memory of that dream in the garden with Ali. Could it possibly come true?

"You think you don't say the right things at the right time, Ram. But you do. At least, with me." She reached over, touching his hand resting on the table near his plate. "I need to be reminded at times like this when things look so dark. You give me hope. Do you realize that? I can't believe it's the same Ram Torres I knew from before. You were hiding such a wonderful side of yourself from all of us."

"If it helps, I'll do it some more." He saw her lower lip tremble and could feel just how emotional she had suddenly become. He'd never seen Ali cry except when she saw a child in danger. It was never about her. She needed to cry now but he was still reluctant to reach out to her.

"What're your plans for today?" he asked, changing the subject. Everyone had been sticking close to home because of Cara's needs.

"I don't have any. I'll check on Cara from time to time, knocking on her door. If she doesn't answer, I won't go in. Sometimes, she'll ask me to come in. Otherwise, I leave her alone."

"It's the right thing to do. Your parents live in a nice neighborhood. Do you ever walk around the area?"

"We have two bikes," she said, brightening. "It would be nice to do something different to break the energy around here. I wonder if Cara would be okay if we left for a little while and did a quick turn around the neighborhood? I know she depends on having you here as her guard dog."

"We wouldn't be gone long and your parents have a radio they can use to contact us if we need to hurry back."

"That sounds great," Ali said, finishing off her eggs. "A fifteen-minute bike ride sounds wonderful, Ram. I really do need to get out of the house for a while."

"So do I." But he had another reason for it. If Ali could have that time with him, she wouldn't be reading that report. Oh, Ram knew that eventually she'd open up her laptop and find it there. He knew she was going to be very upset, and wanted to delay that a bit longer.

"Okay," he said, rising. "I'll clean up in the kitchen. Go change if you need to, write your mother a note, and we'll take off for a bit."

CHAPTER 3

Mid-October
Tucson, AZ

ALI LOVED THE cool morning air as they climbed on two of the bikes stored in the garage, and rode down the wide avenue. It was early, so few cars were on it this time of day. Ram cycled up beside her, remaining on the outside in his protective mode. This time, she didn't bristle over it. In fact, since her return home to the bombshell issues with her sister, she needed someone to do that—protect her. Ram was turning out to be a safe harbor, much to her surprise. He hadn't even complained about riding Cara's ladies bike, such was his security about his own masculinity.

They pedaled along the local streets in easy silence. The neighborhood consisted of many single-story yellow, pink, gray, and pale-green stucco homes with pretty, Spanish red-tile roofs. As they rode, Ali observed the desert landscape that everyone had in their yard. Water was precious, and most Tucson homeowners knew it, choosing xeriscaping instead of planting grass. Their front yards featured desert plants and trees that required little water.

Ali and Ram had agreed to use the fifteen-minute bike ride so he could get a view of the neighborhood from a security perspective. Were there any danger spots? Ram made a few mental notes, and then realized he was having fun with Ali.

She had come to the same conclusion. With the cool, morning air brushing past her face, it was actually enjoyable riding a bike alongside Ram.

"This is the first time you've left the house," Ram said as they turned a corner.

"The last couple of days have been so intense," Ali said. "I wanted to be there if Cara needed me."

"Right now, she probably needs your mother, too."

"You're right. And that's okay, but I can tell how wearing it's becoming for Mama. I worry, Ram. This is all so new to her. She has her limits, too . . . everybody does."

Ram turned the corner onto another wide, quiet neighborhood street, staying abreast of Ali.

"She appears to me to be a very strong woman. And if she is, Mary can handle it."

"My mother is the strongest person I know. You're right about your assessment of her. I'm looking for ways to help Mama, though, Ram. She loves to cook for the family, but I'm going to jump in and help her. Plus, she's on a Yaqui committee and has a lot of responsibility to her people. She's so busy that some days, she's pulled twenty different ways."

"I could tell that by all the phone calls she gets," he said. "I admire her responsibility to her tribe."

"They're her other family. And they're my family, too."

"I heard Mary say that she was getting together a spirit-returning ceremony for Cara. What does that mean? I'm not up on Native American healing."

She smiled a little, enjoying the peaceful exchange with Ram. This was the first time he'd shown interest in her Yaqui background. "Most indigenous people believe that a traumatized person can lose a piece of his or her spirit. That piece has gotten "stuck" in the trauma, leaving the victim feeling as if he or she isn't whole . . . and it's true." She looked over at Ram, who was listening closely.

"That's amazing," he said, his mind racing. The idea of the soul shattering into pieces after a trauma—well, it sounded very possible, even for a non-believer. The imagery certainly hit home.

Ali nodded and went on. "A ceremony can be offered to the Great Spirit or whomever the tribe believes in to 'call' that piece home to the individual. When it comes back, the medicine person blows it back into the person's head and heart, welcoming it back home, asking it to stay. Then, the person doesn't feel disconnected, or as if something was taken from them, or that something is missing any longer. They're whole again and it helps them heal from the trauma much more quickly."

Ram surprised her by giving her a boyish grin. "I must have pieces of my soul scattered all over Afghanistan, then, because I've seen a lot of trauma."

Snorting, Ali said, "You and me both. Our auras probably look like Swiss cheese from a psychic's viewpoint."

"Has your mother ever performed the ceremony for you?"

"Yes, several times."

"Did it work? Did you feel different because of it?"

Ali could see he was trying to grasp the concept and understand it. "Yes, it did work because I felt better afterward, more stable, more 'myself' again."

"Will Cara agree to do it? I'm assuming your

mother has to ask if Cara wants this ceremony done for her?"

"Oh, my mother would never do this without permission. Yes, she did ask Cara and she does want the ceremony. I think it will really help her."

"I hope it does," Ram said. "I truly do."

By the time they returned home, Ali saw that the front door was open. As they walked the bikes up the driveway, she could smell bacon frying. Her mother was up and making breakfast for the others. She was glad she had left a note next to the stove so her mother wouldn't worry about them. They opened the garage door, stowed the bikes, and hung up the helmets nearby.

Now, Ali had to prepare herself for the day ahead. "Thanks for going on that ride with me," she told Ram, halting at the door between the garage and house. "That was a great idea."

He looked up at her. "You look better, and the tension's left your face."

"Thanks to you. Keep talking to me, Ram. I like meeting this side of you." She saw a wicked look come to his eyes. "I mean it. I really do."

Ram smiled a little. "I guess I'm kind of getting used to it a little more every day, Ali. It doesn't feel so hard for me to stay open to everyone. You're being my teacher, too, in another way and I appreciate it."

Ali became quiet, studying him in the silence

that fell softly between them. "When we talked down in Mexico after the mission, I wanted to try and know the real you, Ram." She opened her hands toward him. "I just never dreamed that this was who you are when you're not hiding it."

He gave her an uneven smile. "I'm trying and I want to do it for both of us, Ali."

Her lips curved slightly and she nodded. "It means so much to me that you are trying."

He reached out, lightly touching her hand on the wooden rail of the stairs she stood upon. "That's good to know." He tried to lighten the conversation. "What you need to do is get out of the house more often. Break the energy, as you've said before. It's healthy to do that, Ali. Right now, Cara's fighting her own internal war. We know what that's like because of our own PTSD. She's got to name it, understand it, and learn to live with it. None of that's going to be easy, as we well know."

"I just wish," Ali said, her voice soft, "that of all the people this could have happened to, it hadn't been Cara. She's so unlike a warrior, and I don't know if she has the fighting spirit it takes."

"People are resilient and she might surprise you," he soothed, removing his hand from hers. He'd seen her eyes grow tender when he touched her, so he left his hand in place, understanding it might be giving her nourishment in an emotional sense. And when he lifted it away, he saw her expression sag, as if he was feeding her and she needed what he was sharing with her. Ram wasn't sure about it all because he was still learning himself. "Look, Ali, while all this attention is good for Cara, she's not going to get strong until everyone starts letting her stand on her own two feet. Maybe you can get your mother to come with you to run errands. She needs to get out of the house sometimes, too."

"You're right." She smiled a little, holding his warm gaze. Ram was more than likeable when he was like this. "You're my set of objective eyes. Don't ever be afraid to take me aside and share what you see, please? It helps me recalibrate myself and get back into balance."

Ram gave her an intense, burning look. "I'm here for you, Ali. That's the way it is. I know you don't like me protecting you, but it's who I am. I can't help it if I want to shield you from being hurt."

"I know. I'm getting over my attitude about it. And I appreciate you caring enough to do it for me, despite my previous gripes about it. But do come to me if you want to talk? I'm the first to admit that I'm a hot mess right now."

"I have your back, *princesa*."

The endearment in Spanish touched her as nothing else ever could. Ali stood there, and her heart thudded to underscore what his roughly whispered endearment did to her. Completely caught off guard, she felt Ram invisibly reach out, grazing her cheek with his strong fingers. He'd stood casually at the bottom of the steps, at ease, but she felt a palpable, throbbing coming from him. Ali could feel it clear to her toes and back. She swallowed hard. "Is that how you see me? As a princess?"

His smile was tentative. "I guess in my mind I've always called you that."

"Since when?"

"Since meeting you when you first came into our SEAL team."

Eyes widening, she stood there digesting his explanation. Ram wasn't one to lie. He never had before. Ali knew this was an endearment. It wasn't a military nickname he'd given her. And the way he'd said it, those velvety words entering her heart, felt so good, so right.

She heard her father and mother through the door, speaking in Spanish, and realized it was time to go in and help her mother get breakfast. Lamenting the bad timing, Ali saw Ram watching her, his expression one of curiosity—and something else she couldn't put her finger on. At least, not right now.

"Would you like me to call you that?" he asked as she opened the door. "Or does it bother you, Ali?"

Turning, she looked down at Ram. "I never knew you thought of me that way in the first place. I know it's a loving term, and I'm a bit confused by it . . . and by you."

Shrugging, he said, "You wanted to know the rest of me, right? Well, this is who I am, Ali." He grinned, and his teasing made her feel a tad better.

"I like who I'm with now, Ram. But that's a term for lovers and we aren't lovers." Again, she saw a glint in his eyes, unable to translate it. She also noticed a new gentleness radiating from Ram. *What was going on here?*

Ali didn't have time to analyze this conversation because her father called them to the breakfast table.

"Coming, Papa," she called over her shoulder, opening the door to the kitchen. They'd already had breakfast, but they would sit and chat with the rest of the family as they ate their meal.

ALI FELT ILL after reading Wyatt Lockwood's copy of the DEA debrief from her sister, Cara. After she joined her parents while they ate their breakfast, she'd gone to her room to check her emails, and there it was. She'd felt an icy fist in her stomach as she absorbed its contents. Her first thought was: did Ram read this yet? The copy was addressed to both of them.

It was almost noon, and she felt claustrophobic in her quiet bedroom. She wasn't used to being so confined indoors. Even in her hiding spot in Sonora, she'd had room to move. She couldn't watch the fortress twenty-four hours a day, so she'd gone down the tree, hiked around, looked for other entry spots into the fortress. She was an athletic, outdoorsy person, not a stay-at-home type, like Cara.

Shutting off her computer, she knew she wanted to talk to Ram before doing anything else. Cara had already told everyone she wanted to stay in her room and knit. Knitting was calming for her and Ali was glad her sister had found something to help soothe her ragged emotions. She had refused anti-depressants, anti-anxiety medication, and sleep aids. While Ali agreed in principle, she thought some meds might be helpful in the short term. She felt it might have relieved some of her sister's constant agony and suffering.

She had pulled her hair into a ponytail and changed into a pair of white shorts, flip-flops, and a pale-green tube top. A swamp cooler, a pre-air-conditioning device to keep houses in the Southwest from feeling like frying pans in the summer, cooled the house. She left her room and looked down the hall for Ram. What was he doing? Where was he?

Cara had told everyone that if her door was open, it meant she would receive visitors. If it wasn't, she asked to be left alone. The door was closed. Ram's door, however, was open and Ali peeked in. He wasn't there.

She went out to the garage, just on a hunch. Sure enough, there he was, oiling and greasing the bikes, his fingers coated with the fluid.

"Hey," she called softly from the door, "could you use some company?" She saw amusement in his eyes as he picked up a nearby rag and wiped off his fingers.

"Bored?" he teased.

She shook her head. "No," she said, coming quickly down the stairs after shutting the door. She walked over to stand beside Ram and the bike he was working on. "I just got done reading the debrief on Cara," she admitted, her voice strained. Instantly, Ram sobered and looked up.

"Are you okay, Ali? It was tough to read, even for me."

His caring words were as unexpected as they were welcome, and she felt warmth pouring through her. Ali swore it was like a living cascade of comfort entering and surrounding her. The knot in her stomach eased.

"Actually, I'm not feeling very good, if you want the truth." She saw his eyes soften, and knew that her well-being was a priority for him. In that moment, all she wanted was to walk into his arms and be held.

"How can I help you?" Ram asked tenderly.

She nearly burst into tears, just hearing the tone of his voice over his gently asked question. She whispered, "I just wish . . . "

"What?" Ram asked, turning away from the bike and giving her his full attention.

"Cara had a boyfriend, Colin Stein," she explained, "and she thought she was in love with the guy. I only met him once. I wasn't impressed, but Cara liked him." Pushing tendrils off her cheek, she continued, "He dumped her after she got kidnapped, Ram. I'm so damned angry about what he did I could spit nails."

She watched him set the bike up on the hooks and take the second one down, turning it upside down to work on the chain and the hubs of the wheels.

"Bastard," he muttered.

Her eyes flashed with anger. "Now, when she needs it most, she has no one to hold her as she goes through this, Ram." Her voice broke. "No one . . . "

He stopped working and came around the bike, settling his hands lightly on her slumping shoulders. "She's luckier than most, Ali. She has a loving family supporting her. So many people don't have that luxury. They have to battle a situation alone." He looked up at the ceiling for a moment and then shifted his gaze to hers. "Stein showed his true self, that's all. Better that Cara knows it now than to marry the coward later."

"I guess you're right." She searched his face, drowning in the warmth he was sending her. It felt so good, so steadying, nourishing her in ways she so desperately needed right now. "I know we haven't talked about this, but what do you think of Mama and Papa knowing about the debrief? Do you think it would hurt or help Cara?"

He lifted his hands from her shoulders. "I've thought about that, too. In the long run, even though it will upset them now, they'll be prepared to help her over the long term by knowing exactly what she survived. They won't have to guess about it because she's not telling them, or lie awake at night imagining all kinds of other gruesome scenarios."

She chewed on her lower lip, moving away from him. Ali knew that if she didn't, she was going to ask him to hold her, just for a moment or two. She walked a few feet away, trying to hold onto her eroding composure. "I'm torn, Ram. My folks are already destroyed by this. So is Cara."

"So are you," he said in a low voice, watching her.

Tears burned in her eyes and Ali struggled to get herself under control. She turned away, her head dipping.

Always tuned in to her, Ram suddenly realized the intensity of her emotional state. Quickly, he wiped off his fingers on a nearby cloth, and moved those few feet to where Ali stood with her back toward him. She was hunched over, shoulders down, telling him she was battling a hell of an emotional reaction right now. Who wouldn't be?

He knew approaching Ali from behind wasn't a smart idea. After all, she was an operator. If he put his hands on her shoulders from behind, she'd probably fly into action, muscle memory taking over, thinking she was under attack. Halting, Ram decided to move in a larger circle around her so she could catch sight of him in her peripheral vision.

Ali had her hands pressed against her face and he could hear her taking deep, jerky breaths, trying to remain in control. He saw the glimmer of tears begin to leak through her fingers even though he didn't want to see her crying. Unsure, he stood there for a moment, wanting to comfort her, but afraid she'd reject him if he tried to hold her.

What the hell! He couldn't behave like an emotional coward a minute longer . . .

CHAPTER 4

Mid-October
Tucson, AZ

ALI WAS SO lost in her morass of emotions that she froze for a moment when Ram enclosed her in his embrace. She had hidden her face between her hands, struggling so hard not to sob aloud that she hadn't heard Ram approaching her.

His arms gently wrapped around her shoulders, almost hesitantly, as if silently asking her if she would accept his comfort or not. She was so caught up in her own need of him, of what he was offering, that she automatically stepped deep into his embrace. As she pressed her wet cheek against his t-shirt, she swore she heard him groan, but she couldn't really tell if it was him or her.

Ram's arms tightened around her, drawing her fully against him and she felt his protective, healing energy soothing the storm within her. This wasn't sexual, nor was it a come-on, and she knew it. No, Ram was being sensitive and sympathetic, trying to help her. And that's when the first sob ripped out of her.

The sound was foreign to her, like that of an animal crying out in sheer anguish. As his hand cupped the back of her head, gently holding her as her entire body shook with her weeping, Ali surrendered fully to Ram.

The debriefing memo had been like a can opener ripping her open, and every detail of Cara's kidnapping butchered her heart. She huddled in Ram's arms, absorbing his hand as it glided gently up and down her back, as if to try and take away some of her anguish. She felt his moist breath near her temple, his breathing slow and easy compared to her own. He was like a mountain surrounding her, and it made her feel safe in a way she'd never felt before. Ram's tenderness and thoughtfulness toward her exploded all her previous theories about him as a man, but she was weeping so hard, she couldn't sort anything out right now.

Ram held her as if she were a fragile, priceless gift placed in his care. The sensation, the knowing, was so real that slowly, Ali's sobs lessened, and finally diminished to a point where even her tears stopped flooding from her tightly closed eyes. It was then that she became acutely aware of Ram as a man. Inhaling his scent, it brought her relief from her jagged, roiling emotions. His arms brought her solace, but weren't crushing her against him. Somewhere in her tumbling mind, she realized he was holding her, but not imprisoning her. Overwhelmed with his sensitivity she'd never experienced before, it brought a fresh round of tears. Only this time, she cried for them because they'd gotten off on the wrong foot with one another all those years ago and never seen the goodness the other had to offer. It saddened her in a way that made her feel guilty and she questioned why she'd projected on Ram like that. There was no blame, just an awareness that now, she had been lucky enough to meet the other side of him. While not having many social skills, Ram had a pure, unselfish heart—and she was getting to experience it firsthand.

Staggered by all the sensations, the awareness of Ram as a man who was being kind to her, of her heart clamoring to remain in the safe harbor of his arms, his body huge and protective against hers, Ali stood there in the gathering silence, sponging in what he was unselfishly sharing with her. He was supporting her emotionally in a way that she'd so desperately needed. Most of all, the light skimming of his hand across her shoulders and down her back soothed her immensely, so many of her sharp, jagged emotions calming beneath his ministrations.

She could hear the slow thud of his heart beneath her ear, the fabric of his t-shirt, completely soaked with her tears. If he minded, he said nothing about it. Closing her eyes, Ali couldn't sort all the impressions, the new, awakening feelings in her own heart toward Ram, right now. His hand settled on the center of her back and she felt him give her a bit of a hug and then he released her, although he kept his hands on her upper arms to steady her, just in case.

Looking up through her tear-beaded lashes, Ali saw a new tenderness burning in his eyes. Even his mouth, usually tight in a hard line, was relaxed. "T-thank you . . . " she whispered, her throat still scratchy from crying so much. She suddenly felt fresh tears flow from her eyes again. She opened her hand that rested against his powerful chest. "I-I didn't know you'd do something like this . . . I didn't . . . " She saw him look above her head, the corners of his mouth drawing in for a moment before he lowered his gaze and met hers again.

"A long time ago, when I was a young boy, I had a woman who wasn't my mother hold me after I'd got beaten up by four boys in grade school. I'd never cried in front of anyone until that time, Ali. I had gone to Mazzie because she was teaching me how to read and write English. She saw my black eye and my dirty, bloodied shirt, and opened her arms to me. I was hurting so much that I just walked into them, and she held me. I never cried as hard or as long as I did then."

His mouth moved, as if to hold back a lot of surfacing emotions. When he continued, his voice was low and thick. "I felt as if you were at that point with Cara, with all the loads you're carrying on your shoulders for your entire family. They all look to you for help, for guidance, and suggestions on how to deal with your sister. It's a lot for anyone to carry."

He gave her a slight smile. "I guess I just wanted to let you know that you can lean on me. I have a pretty broad set of shoulders and I can help carry others' loads, too. I'm not the ogre you thought I was."

Wincing at the hurt in his deep tone, she stood inches apart from him, not wanting him to release her arms, not wanting to leave the heat rolling off his massive body, or the sense of shelter that still surrounded her, making her feel steadier, more clear-headed. "I-I'm sorry I didn't see this in you before, Ram. I really am. That was exactly what I needed." She pulled her arm from his hand and reached up, placing her palm over the wet fabric on his shirt where she'd cried. "I've made a mess of your t-shirt, I'm afraid," she added lamely, giving him an apologetic look.

"Don't worry about it, Ali. It will dry."

She had so many questions about what he'd just shared with her. She knew nothing of his background. Ali wanted to pursue it but knew it wasn't a good time. It was all she could do to put herself back together right now. "Thank you for being here for me, Ram."

"No one should cry alone, Ali. Not ever."

She saw a deep flash of pain in his eyes, but then it was gone. Wiping her mouth free of the last of the tears, she let Ram release her and forced herself to move away from him, sitting down on a nearby stool. His concerned gaze followed her. "You're right, no one should cry alone." She gave a sad look at the door that led into the house.

"Cara has no one like you in her life, ever since Colin abandoned her." She swallowed, touching her brow and then sending him a warm look. "But you were here for me. I consider that a gift."

"That's what friends are for in my world, Ali. I know I wasn't much of a friend to anyone on our team."

"You had your reasons."

"The last three years have changed me, I hope, for the better," he said, taking another stool and placing it opposite her, about three feet between them.

Tilting her head, she whispered, "Ram, I have so many questions for you. You just aren't the guy I knew on the team."

"There were other parts of my personality running me at the time, Ali."

"Well," she said, giving him a slight, trembling smile, "I sure like this side of you, instead."

He looked away. "I wasn't sure I should try and hold you at all, Ali. I was expecting you to push me away, get angry, and tell me to never touch you again." He lifted his chin, assessing her reaction to his gruffly spoken words. "We haven't exactly done this before, so I couldn't assume it was what you wanted. But I wanted to try to help you . . . "

Sitting up, her eyes widened. "I wouldn't push you away, Ram. I know what comforting another human being feels like. Your embrace and your approach to me was about that, nothing else. I can tell the difference between sex, flirtation, and a man showing human compassion."

A corner of his mouth lifted slightly. "Yeah, and I was glad you could because all I wanted to do was make you feel better, knowing I was there for you when you really needed it." He gestured toward the door to the house. "You have three people leaning heavily on you, Ali, and I didn't want you to do that alone."

"I believe it, Ram, I really do." She wiped her eyes dry with her fingers. "And I feel better now. Thank you for picking up on what I needed. I hadn't expected it . . . "

She saw hurt enter his eyes, which was the last thing she wanted. Hastily, she added, "Look, this is my fault, not yours, Ram. I was knee-jerking from the past. God, what a pattern we set up with one another. I'm trying to break it and I know you are too. Sometimes," and she pushed dark tendrils that had stuck to her cheek, behind her ear, "I fall into old patterns with you. I don't mean to. I try to stay on top of it." She sighed. "And I don't always succeed. You get hit by me again, but you're not striking back like you used to when I did it. That's what is so different."

"We're both trying. I know that, Ali." He sighed. "Especially under these circumstances. Maybe, if we were back at Artemis, we'd have the time and environment where we could stop those knee-jerk reactions. But here, we're going to stumble and fall sometimes. Look, we both have the hides of a rhino. I'm pretty confident that we'll take each other's trial and errors in stride."

"How did you get so wise about people, Ram?"

Shrugging, he said, "Life 101 gave it to me, I suppose. And you're right: I was a shadow in our team. I grew up like that. It was the only way I knew how to be."

"I thought you were that way because I was a woman coming into your all-male team."

"I was closed up *before* you came in, so this

isn't on you. I remained that way when you were there and after you left us. It had nothing to do with you."

Relief plunged through her. "And all along, I thought it was me making you react the way you did."

"No. It's all mine to own. And I'm sorry you felt responsible."

"In a weird way," she confided, her voice raw with emotions, "knowing that helps me a lot."

"What do you mean, Ali?"

"For all that time, even after I left the team, until just now, I thought it was my fault because you didn't believe a woman in your team could be worth anything."

"Well, to be honest, I did think that at first," he admitted. "But as I got to see you out on ops, I changed my opinion. I grew to trust you out there just like the rest of the guys did. I never had a problem with you out in the field."

"But you did elsewhere? Why?"

He looked uncomfortable, but answered her question as best he could. "It came from my growing up years, Ali. And it was very wrong of me to project the shit that happened in those years on you."

Trying to put the pieces together from what he'd shared earlier with her, Ali's mind spun with fragments of answers from him. "We all project on one another, Ram. That's nothing new. I try to stop it when I catch myself doing it to you or someone else. It's not fair to that person. You're blaming them when they did nothing to you. Is that what you were doing to me?"

Moving around on the stool, Ram chose his words carefully. "I did project on you, because at that time, I was at a place when you were assigned to our team where I was working through a lot of bad feelings toward the person who was really at fault."

"Another woman?" she guessed.

"Yes, it was."

She could feel him not wanting to go anywhere else with this conversation. Ali had no wish to have Ram board back up. "Well," she said gently, opening her hands toward him, "I've been wanting to be held, but I never thought it would be coming from you in my crisis. I'm glad it did."

She saw something flare in his green eyes, a reflective look on his face as he studied her. The silence hung between them, but it was thoughtful, buoyed by their growing closeness. Ali felt so free now that she could talk with Ram without his defensiveness and her reactions in play.

"I'm glad to hear that, Ali. I really am. All I want between us is peace. Maybe, it's time for us to work on a friendship with each other. I'd like that very much."

She looked surprised. "I think we've been

working toward friendship since this mission, Ram. Don't you?"

Nodding, he said, "I guess so. Ali, I've never been friends with a woman before, so this is new territory for me. I'll probably stumble around and make a lot of mistakes with you in the process. Are you ready for that?"

She grinned a little, rubbing her hands down her thighs. "Ram, you have nothing to worry about on that score. After all the kindness and support you've shown me and my folks . . . come on!" She saw relief and pride in his expression, as if that was exactly what he needed to hear from her. Ali realized Ram wanted to hear how she felt a lot more often than she was volunteering. He was like every human being—needing honest compliments so he'd feel good about himself. It would build his confidence, and best of all, create a bridge of trust between them. Never had she wanted anything more than to create that connection between herself and Ram.

He looked vulnerable, more like a little boy right now as they spoke to one another honestly, without holding back, for the first time.

"I like starting over with you," he admitted gruffly.

"Friendship is a good objective for us to work toward," she agreed softly. "I'd love that to happen for us."

"Me, too." Ram sat up, pulling his shoulders

back, as if to get rid of some accumulated, invisible tension he carried. "I can be a good friend to you, Ali."

"You already are," she whispered, her voice filled with rising emotion. "You're making it a lot easier for me to open up to you, Ram. I really need that in a relationship."

"I'll try to stay that way for you," he promised. "But I'll have my moments, too. I hope you can be patient with me, Ali."

She got off the stool and came over, throwing her arms around his shoulders, giving him a swift, strong hug. Ram stiffened for a moment, and then relaxed in her embrace, as if never expecting that from her. Stepping back a few feet, she said, "I'm so glad you're offering this to me, Ram. I never needed it more than right now."

He kept his hands on his thighs and held her gaze. "I think I'm reading you right, Ali. I have to admit, I'm not always sure what's appropriate between us. Like earlier," and he hitched a thumb across his shoulder where he had held her in that embrace, "I wasn't sure what was the right thing to do to help you. I knew I wanted to be there, to comfort you, but I wasn't sure you'd even accept me holding you. This was only the second time it's happened between us." He wanted to add that their kiss in the cave in Sonora had given him the courage to reach out to her once more, but decided against it.

She sighed and her lips compressed for a moment. The look in Ram's eyes broadcast his unsureness. "We can talk, Ram. We can ask one another if we want to be held. This is on both of us. I wanted you to hold me so badly earlier, but I was chicken. I didn't have the guts to ask you to because of our past. I wanted your arms around me." She gave him a tender glance. "And somehow, you cut through all that past we'd accumulated, saw what I needed and had the courage to just do it. You didn't let the past stop you."

"Yeah, well, what if in the future I read you wrong, Ali? What then?"

"We both will misread one another," she promised. She reached out, briefly touching his heart with her fingers across the expanse of his t-shirt. "You have a wonderful heart-centered GPS that unerringly knows what someone needs, Ram. You need to just keep trusting that sense. I need to play catch up, but I'll get there."

Ali withdrew her fingers. "I promise I'll do my best to make this work between us. You're very important to me." And she stopped, because she didn't dare tell him any more than that. If Ram at all suspected her vivid, sexual dreams about them in bed, sharing white-hot intimacy, laughter, and good feelings, he'd probably back off in shock.

Ali was sure all the feelings were on her side,

and that had to remain her secret. She would cherish any positive relationship with Ram and be grateful for whatever it turned out to be. It was far better than what they'd shared before, that was for damn sure. Anything was better than that toxic stew that had bubbled between them.

"You're important to me too, Ali. Let's keep talking. We need times like this alone and away from everyone. It will also help us be strong for your family if we're strong for one another. And we're sharing other good things that make us feel stable, comfortable, and complete. It doesn't get any better than that, does it?"

CHAPTER 5

November 10
Tucson, AZ

RAM DISCOVERED DURING his three weeks with the Monteros that his favorite place to hang out was in the garage. He was good with mechanics, and had already fixed Diego's lawn mower, his weed whacker, and installed a new electric fan in Mary's kitchen for her stove. He also liked being in Tucson because Ali was here, along with her warm, vibrant family. Because he'd never grown up in this kind of family environment, he was enjoying being part of Ali's.

Cara, who was struggling with post-kidnapping trauma, was still indoors, usually in her room. He knew everyone reacted to trauma differently, and given that Cara was a person of a more delicate nature, he understood her fear of walking outdoors. She'd been kidnapped while walking down a neighborhood street in the late afternoon, and was still afraid of exposure to male strangers. She refused to take a short walk, even with Ram and Ali at her side, and didn't even want to go into her own backyard and work in the garden. At least, not yet.

Taking out his carving knife, Ram decided to use this time to create a wood sculpture. These moments brought him the greatest pleasure and solace. Right now, Cara was out in the living room, knitting, and Ali was keeping her company. Mary was at a meeting at the reservation and Diego was at the pecan farm, where he worked as the manager.

His mind, hell, his heart, was now squarely centered on Ali. Since the day he'd had the guts to hold her when she needed to cry her heart out, everything had changed—remarkably, in fact. Did he want her friendship? Of course. But he wanted more than that, if he was honest with himself. He wanted *her* in his bed, in his arms— forever.

After having had a taste of how good he felt after opening up to Ali, he hungered for more intimate talks with her. Their last one had filled him with such hope, he was still on a high days later. And his feelings certainly went far beyond the "friendship" she'd proposed.

He was learning all kinds of fascinating things about Ali, too. She had taken him to her bedroom one day to show him the four shelves of horse statues made out of glass, metal, and plastic that she'd collected since childhood.

After that, whenever he could find a few moments, Ram was out in the garage, away from prying eyes, creating a horse sculpture from the ribs of the saguaro cactus. Diego had given him permission to use them because he had no use for the small pieces. He was thrilled with the idea and admired Ram's woodworking skills.

Ram kept the horse he was working on under wraps. He always placed a dusty canvas cloth around it and hid it in one of Diego's tool drawers, where Ali was less likely to stumble upon it. Every chance he got, he tried to come out here and do some work on it. Slowly, the horse was taking shape. It filled him with happiness to be doing this as a surprise for her. Ali had no idea that he loved carpentry and woodcarving.

Ali . . . his heart swelled with a deep yearning for her company. Over the last two weeks, Cara had needed her more than anyone else. As a result, he and Ali had spent a lot less time together. Ram was acutely aware of how drained Ali looked during the evening meals the family took together. On the plus side, Cara was now eating with all of them. It was a sign that she was emerging from the darkness within her, and beginning to heal from the kidnapping and assault.

From his own experience with PTSD, Ram could often tell where Cara was on any given day with her healing journey. But right now, he was focusing on Ali's state of mind, concerned that she needed a breather. He wanted to get her out of the house for a while, both for a change of scenery and for a chance to get some alone time with her.

Ali, as the older daughter, took on way too much responsibility for the whole family, Ram had discovered.

The door behind him opened, and twisting around to look over his shoulder, he saw it was Ali. "Hey, what's up?" he asked, setting his carving knife aside and discreetly pulling the canvas cover over his secret project.

"I needed a time out. Want some company? I know you need your quiet time, too."

He grinned and gestured to her. "Sure, come on in. I was just thinking the same thing." He got up, placing the project in the drawer and shutting it.

"Great!" Ali breathed, closing the door and giving him a grateful look.

"Come on over," he invited, pulling out another stool and placing it near his own. Ram enjoyed watching her walk over to the large counter where he sat. Today, Ali had her long, black hair in a set of braids, and looked a lot like her mother. With the cooler, fall weather, Ali had changed her shorts for jeans. She wore sneakers and bright red socks to match her long-sleeved red tee. The jeans weren't tight on her, but his body responded anyway. Ali had that effect on him, which he didn't want her to see. For her, their relationship was about friendship, not lust and sex.

Ali came to a halt a foot away from him. "Papa said you were figuring out some electrical issues with Mama's under-the-cabinet lights she's always wanted."

No one except Diego knew he was making the saguaro horse for Ali, and he had promised to keep it a secret. Like the well-trained black-ops guy he was, Ram always made sure another project was on the counter. In this case, he had electric wire and ten small lights to show her. "Yeah, I need to make up a whole string of lights. Your mother's kitchen is in an L-shape, so I'm working on measurements," he said, gesturing toward what would probably look like a rat's nest to anyone but another electrician.

She raised her brows, looking at all the wiring and the different colors of each wire strand. "Looks kind of complicated."

"Not really. It probably looks chaotic to most people," he said, picking up a red wire, "but I can see a simple blueprint in front of me."

Snorting, Ali chuckled. "You're right about it

looking chaotic."

He set the wires back down and nudged them into place. "How are you doing?" He looked up at her, seeing the darkness in her beautiful golden eyes. Someday, he wanted to kiss those eyelids of hers, smell and taste the sweetness of her skin beneath his lips. Would such a day ever come? Ram didn't know, but since being here with Ali, it was all he dreamed about at night. His old dreams—nightmares, actually—had been replaced by dreams of the two of them together, happy and fulfilled.

Ali was changing him for the better, but he could also see his impact on her. Every day, they became a little more open to one another. A little closer, a bit more intimate and sharing.

"Cara is going through a down period," she said. "She just left for her bedroom to go and lie down. I think she's depressed again."

"It happens," Ram murmured. He reached out, patting her shoulder gently. "Hang in there. She *is* getting better even if it's incrementally. Rome wasn't built in a day." How badly he wanted to do more than reassure her. His vivid, lusty dreams of loving Ali occurred almost nightly. It was a bitch waking up with a hard-on, sweaty as hell, his heart aching for her to be at his side. He squeezed her shoulder briefly and then removed his hand. Never did he want Ali to think his friendship with her meant he really wanted to have sex with her. He was well aware of how women took a man's touch. He'd had plenty of women in his jaded past and understood exactly what kind of touch meant a promise of pleasure to come.

Ram rarely reached out to touch, because he was always tentative about what she might think, and how far to go. But he had noticed that lately, when he did, Ali's eyes lightened and he felt her responding in the best of ways to him, the tension leaving her body. He was learning by doing, and then watching the result of his friendly intimacy with her. How Ram wished it was much more than that, but even this was pleasurable and made his heart swell with happiness.

Ali sighed and sat down on the other stool, pulling one leg across her other knee. "I know. Most days, I can handle it. But today, I felt like a wild animal pacing in a cage as I sat talking with her. She repeats the same stuff, Ram. Over and over again. I don't even think she knows she's doing it."

"Broken record kind of thing," he agreed. "I've seen other guys with PTSD repeat the same description of an op, or a specific event, over and over again." He gave her an amused look. "I'll bet we can look back on our own traumas and see that we were repeating things early on in our healing process, too. Don't you?"

She nodded, and said, "No wonder some

loved ones go bat shit crazy dealing with someone with PTSD," she grumped unhappily. "I've
seen so many divorces happen because of it."

"It can certainly put an awful strain on a mar-
riage," Ram agreed.

"I guess I never saw outside of myself until
just now with Cara going through it. Geez, talk
about being boarded up! I've always prided
myself on being sensitive to other people's needs,
but I guess I'm not, really. The PTSD can
infiltrate me in such a way that I don't see it
happening. But I see it in Cara, so I know I must
be doing it too."

"It's easier to see what's wrong in another
person than ourselves," he said enigmatically,
moving the wires and putting them in a certain
alignment with one another.

"You're so right," Ali muttered. "I don't see
myself as well as I thought."

"It's a process. We're all going through it to
some extent," he soothed. Ram saw how
exhausted she was because she no longer tried to
hide how she felt from him. There was something wonderful about trust, he was discovering.
"Hey, I got an idea I've been mulling around the
past week and I want to pass it under your wolf
nose."

Ali perked up. "Oh? What?"

"Well, actually two things. First, I know that
my time here at the house is coming to an end.

Wyatt called me the other day and said he needs me back for some planning missions about the situation brewing in Mexico. I'm the lead analyst for anything relating to that area."

"Oh, I see." She frowned. "When do you have to leave?"

She seemed to deflate, hearing the news. "Probably in a week. But I have an idea, Ali."

"What?"

"Your sister needs to feel safe here in the house, which is why I'm here. But if I leave, I'm afraid it might create a setback, since she considers me her big, bad security guard dog. I told Wyatt that Cara needed a PSD, a private security detail, who could come and take my place, He could be here for her so she'll continue to feel safe."

"That's a great idea, Ram," Ali said slowly, mulling over the idea.

"Do you agree with me that Cara needs a PSD?"

"Absolutely. Even though I'm a PSD to her, she sees me as her sister, not as a guard. There's a difference in Cara's mind, and it isn't logical, but she's still caught up in the emotions of her capture. I definitely think Delos Charities should pay for a contractor to be here for Cara."

"I'm sure they will. She is getting better, and I'd hate to see her have a setback."

"Yes, she's slowly improving. And Mama and

Papa are adjusting to it, too. Everyone is more relaxed and that's a good thing."

"I told Wyatt the same thing. I have a guy in mind, an old friend of mine, a combat medic who's got a gentle touch. He was on our rescue team—Tyler Hutton? He was with SEAL Team One at J-bad, too."

Instantly, Ali brightened. "Tyler? Sure I remember him! He wasn't on our team, but in J-bad with another team, then he worked on missions with us. He used to help me out in the villages giving medical aid. And he was so wonderful to the women after we got them out of Azarola's villa." She had formed a special relationship with the combat medic, more like a brother to her. Sometimes, both teams went out on an op together and he was someone who could be trusted and counted upon.

"Yes," Ram said, pleased that Ali was positive about the ex-combat medic. "What do you think? Could it be a good match between Cara and him, personality-wise?"

"Oh, yes," she gushed, suddenly excited. "He's such a gentle soul, Ram. He's a great listener. He's so easy going. Unlike us." She managed a twisted grin of amusement. "I mean, I know he was an operator, like us, in the field, but his personality is way different because he's a medic at heart. He loves helping people."

"Good, I'm glad my suggestion is right on

for Cara."

"He's got PTSD just like the rest of us, though. And with his medical powers of observation, he'd be perfect to fill your boots. He'd be able to know exactly how to deal with Cara on any given day. I think it's a great fit. What did Wyatt say about your suggestion?"

"He's gonna ask Tyler, who just got off an op in Peru, if he wants this assignment."

"What about his wife? How would she feel about that?"

"Ex-wife." Shrugging, Ram said, "You know how PTSD screws up a family—well, his wife couldn't handle it, and they divorced a couple of years ago."

"I'm sorry to hear that. I know how much Tyler loved Lisa. That's a shame."

"All part of our business, I guess," he muttered.

"I'll be really bummed to see you go, Ram. We're getting along so well, and you've helped me so much. I'm going to miss you terribly. You've been my sounding board, my safe place to go to blow off my worries and steam."

"I had another thought about that, Ali."

"You're just full of ideas today, aren't you?" she laughed.

"Wyatt said he'd asked you to join Artemis. He's wanted you to come in for an official interview. He can use someone like you in

Mission Planning."

"I told him if things changed with Cara, I'd see him officially about a possible job with Artemis. He said I was already hired and that I would be welcomed any time I wanted to go back to work."

"Good, I'm glad to know that you're an employee," he grinned, looking around the garage. "We get along here. I don't see how we can't get along there. Do you?" Now, her eyes lit up.

"Yes, we're getting along really well," she admitted.

"Yes. He made no bones about getting you to work with us. And why would he? You're one of the top female operators in the world. You bring a lot to their table, Ali, and Wyatt knows that. You were in his team before. He has a long memory and wants only the best of the best for Artemis."

"I told him I wanted that job," she admitted hesitantly. "I know I can't stay here forever. I've got a lot of debt piling up and I need to start working again."

"Well, why not call Wyatt and tell him that? Find out where he sees you in their organization and give him a time frame of when you might start to work."

Looking toward the house, she said, "I worry about Cara, though. If both of us left, it might destabilize her."

"That's why I thought of Tyler. If he agrees to come out here, he'd take both our places. You know how good he is with people. I also think that Mary and Diego would love him like a son, too."

She rubbed her brow. "It's a lot to think about, Ram."

"I've got one more week here, Ali. I'm already tasked with working up missions with Wyatt on Mexico-related ops while I'm still here in Tucson."

"But you went out in the field to help rescue Cara."

He gave her an intense look. "I volunteered for it because she's your sister, Ali. I remember how you used to talk about your family, show pictures to everyone, and tell them stories of your childhood. When Wyatt offered me the lead on that mission, I wanted to take it."

"But you didn't have to," she said slowly, frowning. "You could have had someone else do it. And given our past history, why did you take it, Ram?"

"There's a lot I'd like to share with you, Ali. Cara has been our focus, which is where it should remain for now."

"And when I come back to work for Artemis?" she demanded.

"Then, we'd have the time to continue getting to know one another under less stressful circumstances."

Ali digested his words, feeling as if there was so much more he wanted to say, but Ram was right: this wasn't the time or place. "Well," she said, thinking out loud, "if Tyler agrees to replace you, maybe I could stay on here for another two or three weeks, making sure that Cara's stable and that she transfers her trust from me to him."

"I think Wyatt will do whatever you need under the circumstances, and if you feel better about waiting to see how Tyler works out, tell Wyatt that. I'm sure he'd be okay with it."

Rubbing her chin, Ali said, "Okay . . . that sounds good, Ram. Thanks for having my back on this."

"I'll always have your back, Ali."

She gave him a tender look as she slid off the stool. "You've been more than good on your word. Listen, I'm going to call Wyatt, see what his plan is for me, and decide a time to start to work."

"Let me know how it goes?"

"I promise."

There was a gleam in Ram's eyes she couldn't interpret, although she wished she could. As she padded through the quiet house, picking up on the familiar scents and surroundings that had always made her happy, she felt her heart being tugged in a new direction.

Worry gnawed at her because of her concern

about Cara's unpredictable state. She was much better than before—at least now she was sleeping somewhat at night, and her nightmares were slowly receding. The stress and strain on her parents, however, was constant. She'd tried hard to dispel some of their worry by explaining PTSD, but they still looked confused when they'd discuss it. They weren't the first parents to wrestle with a child who was now an adult, coming home with PTSD.

As she went to her bedroom, she checked first to see that Cara's door was shut, and then closed her own bedroom door quietly behind her. Maybe Tyler was exactly what Cara needed at this point in her recovery. He wasn't a Latino, but he had the heart of one. He was family oriented, loved children, and was gentle with his patients. He emanated kindness, and Ali hoped that Cara would respond to it, trusting him as she trusted her own sister and Ram.

Her bills *were* mounting up and the pressure to get a job had been hitting her the last two weeks. When she'd finally coughed up the problems and stresses to Ram, she'd seen him become concerned. But he was an operator and as such, they fixed things. Maybe telling Wyatt that she might be available soon was his way of helping her fix her mounting bills issue.

Or was it something more? Ali wouldn't call Ram sneaky, but all operators worked well on that slippery chessboard called the shadows. They were operators because they had a fix-it mentality, and were creative in covert ops precisely because of that skill.

With Ram lending his highly regarded opinion toward a potential hire, Ali knew Wyatt wanted her, no questions asked. She had an impeccable reputation in the world of operators. And Ram, she would bet money, had lobbied enthusiastically on her behalf, too, when she'd went back the last time, although he'd probably never admit it.

Sitting down at her small desk, she picked up her cell phone. Ram had her back, and she was deeply grateful for that. Still, Ali worried about her little sister. There was so much at stake. If Tyler couldn't or wouldn't take this assignment to replace Ram, it could hurt Cara's slow-but-sure progress.

And even if Tyler did take the mission, Cara might not take to him. And that would leave Ali holding the bag in the family—again. Sometimes, she grew weary of it, but she wasn't a quitter. She'd do something to make money, and remain at the house to give Cara the stability she needed and the support her parents silently asked of her. Family was family.

As she dialed Wyatt's number, she closed her eyes, feeling her heart trying to adjust to the idea that Ram was leaving soon. He had become so important to her, like a safe harbor when she needed one. He was there. He was always there, someone she could rely upon.

How had he become so indispensable to her life?

The realization hit her fully, and she forced herself to put it aside—for now.

"Wyatt here."

Ali stuffed down her rising emotions and focused on talking with her old chief. "Wyatt? Ali here. I'm calling to talk to you about that job you offered me at Artemis. I have some details to hammer out with you, but I'm ready to be on the payroll."

CHAPTER 6

November 10
Tucson, AZ

RAM WAS IN the kitchen installing the new lights beneath Mary's kitchen cabinets when Ali came wandering in. It was nearly three o'clock, and the house was quiet. Diego and Mary wouldn't be home until six. Cara had her door closed, so it meant she didn't want to be disturbed, or she was sleeping.

Glancing up, he saw that Ali's face was wreathed in thought. "Caught in the act," he teased. Straightening, he said, "Want to do the honors? Flip it on and see if they work?" He gestured to the nearby switch.

He saw Ali instantly respond to his light-hearted tone, her gaze softening on him. The sense of their growing intimacy was always just below the surface—a feeling that never left him.

"Sure," she said, coming over. "Ready?"

"Yep," he said, stepping away from the counter, hands on his hips.

Ali flipped on the switch and instantly the entire counter beneath the cabinets was aglow. "Wow, this is great, Ram!"

He peered beneath the L-shaped circuit hidden beneath the pecan-wood cabinets, making sure everything was in order. "The light is evenly distributed. That's good." He halted at the other end of the counter after checking every light. Straightening, he looked over at Ali. "Well, do you think Mary will like them when she comes home tonight?"

"Oh," Ali intoned, grinning happily, "she'll be like a duck being put back into the water. Thank you for doing this, Ram. It's something my father hasn't gotten around to because he's not an electrician and they can't really afford one."

He smiled and went over to the small toolbox sitting on the counter near Ali. "I like doing things like this," he admitted. "It's one way I can help Mary. She works so hard and the kitchen is pretty dark. This should brighten things up."

"She'll love them," Ali assured him. "Hey, do you have a minute?" Looking toward the entrance, she wanted to make sure Cara couldn't hear them.

"Sure. Shall we go out into the garage?"

Nodding, she said, "Yes, let's go."

Once out there, Ram brought her stool over to his workbench area and sat down a few feet away from her. She seemed to be bursting to tell him something. "Did you call Wyatt?" he wondered, folding his hands between his legs, facing her.

"Yes, and it was a very fruitful conversation, Ram. First of all, thanks for putting a bug in Wyatt's ear about hiring me. He admitted you came to him sometime back, asking if you could find me and offer me a job."

"It was my pleasure, Ali. You'd be a real asset there."

"Everything we talked about earlier, I covered with him. I also discussed Tyler Hutton with him."

"Oh, good. Has he been able to connect with Tyler more personally yet?"

"Yes." She shot him a look of pure relief. "He's interested in taking Cara's personal security detail position, Ram." She clasped her hands to her breast. "I was so hoping he would say yes. And he did."

"That's great! It'll be a big load off your shoulders, Ali."

"Believe me, I know that better than most," she said passionately. "I'm just so relieved, Ram. You can't know how much."

"She's your baby sister," he teased, "And we both know your folks and Cara will like Tyler a lot. The man doesn't make enemies, only friends."

"I agree with you. I'm feeling so much more hopeful about this situation, now."

"I like making you happy, Ali. It's nice to do something that makes you smile like that." He saw her face melt with a look that spiked his body's interest. Ram usually knew when a woman looked at him with sexual interest, but he told himself he was wrong this time. After all, Ali never flirted with him, never signaled in any way that she was interested in him that way. It had to be his imagination, which was pretty active lately.

Every day spent around Ali for the past three weeks was increasing his need for her in every way, not just sexually. This was a first for him. In many ways, Ali was bringing him new experiences, and new ways of looking at his responses to women. Well, at least this woman!

She sighed and gave him a wistful look. "Some days, I feel like the universe is laughing at us. On one hand," she gestured toward the closed garage door that led into the kitchen, "Cara is going through this nightmarish experience, trying to find herself again, fighting every day to get better. And here we are: happy with one another, rediscovering one another on a completely new playing field, not knowing how much goodness was stored beneath our collective surface. Every day has been a pleasant surprise for me, Ram."

"Darkness and light often live together, Ali. You can't have one without the other. You can't separate them, either. You learn to live with what's good and bad within each of us. It's a personal choice and every person has to make it."

"Oh, now you're being a philosopher again, Torres. That's a side to you I didn't even know existed until recently," she teased.

He chuckled. "Sometimes I get into that space. Yeah, but not often." Her sweet smile melted him. "Don't forget, we went through a darker time together before we discovered the light in each other. We've paid a lot of dues to reach this point, don't you think?"

He saw her become thoughtful, studying him in the lulling silence that often occurred between them. Part of it, Ram knew, was the black-ops mentality. One did not just speak on the fly or react quickly. Everything said or seen was carefully assessed through that operator's mind, thoroughly looked at with logic, not emotion, before a decision or a word was uttered.

Ram appreciated that about both of them. Ali took what he said seriously and ran it through her mental software, just as he did with anything she shared with him.

"What *other* sides are there to you?" she demanded, partly smiling, digging intently into his gaze. "What else aren't you sharing with me, Ram?"

"I dunno," he said, shaking his head, mystified. "For whatever reason, Ali, you bring out sides to me I didn't even know existed until you prodded me with your stick." He grinned at her, and was rewarded by her widening smile.

"You're a warrior, a peacemaker, and a philosopher."

"Only with you," he demurred. "I've never shown those sides to anyone else."

Tilting her chin, she asked, "Why not?"

"Because I trust you, Ali. We've gotten to know each other more and more. You've saved my life a number of times. For sure, you've always had my back. Maybe I'm old enough now to start learning to trust and open up to you because I know you're not going to kill me."

She laughed out loud. "You're certifiable, Torres! I swear."

"Thank you. Coming from you, that's music to my ears. I like our times together like this. I know we haven't had many, but I value them so much. I always feel good afterward because I can toss anything at you, and you deal with it perfectly. You don't get defensive or angry at me."

"No, that part of me is gone forever when it comes to you," she said seriously. "Nothing good came from it. Maybe we had to go through it in order to find the honey of our real selves with one another. I don't know."

"You're honey all right," he said. "You have a sweet smile when you're not in combat, you know that?"

Her gaze lifted shyly. "Yeah, well I can say the same for you. I'm sure you wouldn't like being called 'sweet,' but I'm seeing your softer side now. It means so much to me, Ram. Since coming home to Tucson, we've not had one spat, nor have we become defensive with one another."

"I think its age and maturity finally showing up. I hope at this point you consider me a friend. Have I passed that test with you, Ali?"

Her response was immediate—warm and grateful.

"You've been a wonderful friend to me." She grew sober. "I'm going to miss you terribly when you have to leave, Ram. Who will I have to talk to like this after you're gone?"

"Call me," he urged. "Did you give Wyatt a time frame for coming to work at Artemis?"

"He's made it clear he'd like to hire me. He said he wants me in the Mission Planning department, with you. There's so much going on in Mexico that he wants my contacts and all the asset intel I've gleaned over the years down there. He even offered me a huge starting salary, Ram. I thought I heard him wrong the first time he mentioned it."

"I started out at two-hundred-thousand a year," he confided.

She gave him a startled look. "That's what he's offering me! That's *twice* the amount a security contractor usually gets out in the real world."

"Artemis hires only the best," he told her seriously, "and they're willing to pay their people the highest salaries in the industry without blinking an eye. So, when are you coming back for the official meeting with him?"

"I told him I wanted to wait until Tyler gets here to replace you, and then see how Cara's adjusting to him for two or three weeks after that. He said the job is open and there's no drop-dead date for when I have to take it. Wyatt is a stand-up dude. He's sensitive and family oriented, thank goodness."

"Yeah, he really is and so is his wife, Tal. They've made Artemis a family-friendly company. I think you'll like working there with all of us, Ali."

She studied him, giving him a sad look. "I'll miss you, though, dammit."

"At least we aren't fighting anymore," he noted. "And who knows? Maybe in a month, you'll be back East to take the job. By then, you'll be looking for a place to live and I'd be happy to help you with that."

"I'd love your help, Ram. Thanks."

"I had another idea."

"Uh, oh," she laughed, "What now?"

"Well," he hedged, "about three weeks ago, you showed me your collection of horses in your room. I never realized how much you loved riding horses until then."

"It was one of those things I learned as a kid. When my father worked at a large farm outside of Tucson, they had horses. I was riding with him from the age of three, and both Cara and I always had horses available to us. We used to ride like wild children around that five-thousand-acre pecan farm, flying up and down the tops of the huge water ditches around it. I loved riding bareback, feeling the wind tearing at me as we galloped around."

"I like hearing about your younger years," he murmured. "So here's my idea. You were looking really tired the other day because Cara's been leaning heavily on you. So I called up a stable south of Tucson, in Tubac. They offer half-day picnic rides out to the Santa Rita Mountains, which are nearby. We can rent the horses and either ride with a guide or ride by ourselves. I'd like to take you on a picnic-lunch ride to a place called Cottonwood Canyon. Would you like that?" He instantly saw a gleam of excitement flare in her gold eyes. Yeah, he'd pushed her buttons all right and he couldn't help but grin.

"That would be terrific! When did you want to do it?"

"How about this Friday? Your mother is home all day and Cara will have someone here with her. We'll only be about an hour from Tucson if Cara needs us."

"I think she's steady enough to deal with us being gone half a day," Ali said. "Cara's climbing back up again, getting more stable. It'll probably last four or five days, and she likes us to take some time off when she's in that cycle. She's becoming more sensitive to other people, and she knows we need a break. I believe she'll be fine about us going, but I'll ask her and make sure."

"Cara's doing very well," Ram agreed. "I know she has setbacks, but with the kind of support she has around her, she's getting stronger each day."

"Then, let's do it! I'm so excited! It's been ten years since I last threw a leg over a horse, Ram. A half-day ride is going to have me walking like a wishbone afterward."

He laughed at the imagery. "Okay, I'll make the reservation. We'll have to pack our own lunch."

"Leave it to me. I already have some great stuff for a picnic."

"Sounds good," he agreed.

"Okay, Ram, I'm going to go see if Cara is

available. I need to see what she thinks of our plan."

"Good luck!" Ram watched her slide off the stool, turn, and quickly take the concrete steps up to the kitchen. She disappeared inside and quietly closed the door behind her.

He absorbed her child-like excitement, privy to yet another facet she'd never revealed before. There was something touching and beautiful about Ali blossoming, opening one petal at a time, in front of him. Her trust in him was deep now.

Ram knew his own trust wasn't there yet, but he was slowly moving forward. Ali deserved only the truth from him and that was what he was hedging on. How could he ever tell her the truth of his pseudo family? His childhood? Ram cautioned himself to allow things to continue to just organically unfold between them. This wasn't something he could time or rush.

Like everything else they had revealed to one another, it had just naturally happened and it felt right at the time.

Worry seeped into him. If he did share with Ali about his young life, how would she react? The shame and humiliation was still with him to this day, no matter how much he tried to ignore it. Now, with their feelings deepening and growing into a stronger relationship, honesty was the only path for him to take with her. He wouldn't shy away from the truth about what had happened to him, but it scared the hell out of him to even talk about it to her. He was afraid of Ali judging him.

How would she see him afterward? He agonized. She might no longer see him as the consummate hero he wanted to be for her. Ram couldn't stop himself when it came to protecting Ali. Sure, he knew she could defend herself, but dammit, this instinctive urge to protect her came from so deep within, he couldn't tell where it started or ended.

Turning to happier thoughts, he hoped that Cara would give them the green light to go on the horseback ride and picnic. He really liked Ali's sister and admired her spirit in tackling this terrible trauma.

He'd never met anyone quite like her before, but then, the military drew people who already had a lot of inner strength, reserve, and endurance—like Ali and himself.

His memories surfaced. All the women in the brothel were strong and resilient fighters, too. But the ones who had cared for him, who had raised him, had hearts of gold beneath that rhino hide. They knew how to nurture him, hold him, and smother him with kisses until he giggled and tried to escape their cuddling. But he'd loved every second of it, starved for genuine human touches, embraces, and affection that didn't happen that often, but he wished it had.

Those were strong women, unlike Cara. He would never forget any of those wonderful women, especially Mazzie, whom he'd considered his "true" mother. She loved him more fiercely than anyone else at the brothel, and had protected him with that mother-bear personality of hers. Yet, she could instantly melt and become loving and caring when he desperately needed it.

In some ways, Ram thought Ali had a lot of Mazzie's attributes. She was a fierce warrior, too, but when they went into the Afghan villages and she was around the babies and children, Ali had melted into a wonderful, warm mother hen. He'd seen the children turn on like little light bulbs in her presence, their eyes shining as she took as many as she could into her opening embrace. Then, she'd squeeze the daylights out of them until they all shrieked and giggled with laughter.

Love transcended any tongue. It was a universal language, as Ram had discovered. Those kids had all loved Ali, and waited to see if the next SEAL team coming in to help them included her. If it didn't, they pouted, sulked, and asked some of the SEALs where Ali was. They didn't realize she was only with Wyatt's team, and not the others who cruised through their area.

Ali made him feel good, just as she had the kids. Oh, she had only kissed him once, and they had only embraced each other a few times, but her smile was urging his heart to open.

Now, she was beaming the same affectionate smile she had shared with the Afghan children, just for him, and he felt bathed in its sunlight. The closer they became, the more Ali smiled and the wall lowered between them. Her curving lips lifted him, fed him hope, and promised him a dream he could never see coming true. But he dreamed it anyway.

CHAPTER 7

November 10
Tucson, AZ

ALI HALTED AT Cara's open door, knocking lightly on it as she peeked inside. Her sister was sitting in her rocking chair in the corner, knitting. Her black hair, slightly curled at the ends, fell around her shoulders, framing her face. Ali looked for signs of stress first, around Cara's shapely mouth and at the corners of her dark brown eyes. To Ali's relief, she looked at peace for once.

"Want some company?" she asked, standing in the doorway.

Cara lifted her heart-shaped face, giving Ali a warm look of welcome. "Sure, come on in. Look, I'm knitting this for Alberto, my little six-year-old at the kindergarten. His favorite color is red. What do you think?"

"I think you're a genius at knitting," Ali said honestly. "When Mama taught us when we were ten, you took to it. I was a flop at it." Ali came over and touched the proffered, half-finished red sweater. "It feels so soft! I'm sure he'll love getting this." Ali knew that every year, Cara knitted a new sweater for each of her children at school because they tended to outgrow the old ones very quickly. Their families could never afford sweaters of this quality. Most of them were illegal immigrants, and work was hard to find. They lived in the shadows of sprawling Tucson, going to food missions weekly to supplement their diets.

"Alberto's growing like a weed," Cara sighed. "Such a beautiful young boy with black hair and lovely, brown doe-like eyes." Her knitting needles flew back and forth, creating another row on the nearly finished sweater.

Ali sat down on the edge of the bed. On bad days, Cara looked disheveled, her bed remained unmade, her hair uncombed, and she didn't take care of herself. Those were the days when Ali knew depression had captured her spirit.

Today, she wore lightweight, tan wool slacks and a pretty white, long-sleeved blouse with a Victorian lace collar, showing off her beauty, her slender, long neck and the golden hue of her skin. "You must have had a good night's sleep," Ali guessed.

"Yes. I only woke up once and then I fell right back to sleep. No nightmares, no dreams, Ali. I feel so lucky." She stopped knitting, folding her hands in her lap across the sweater. "And you know what? Today I really feel like going back to work. I just figured out I need something to distract me from my own imagination. If I go back to Delos Charity Kindergarten, I can focus on my children, not myself."

"There's some wisdom in doing that," Ali agreed, surprised and hopeful to hear Cara's thoughts about returning to work. "But are you up to a full day of teaching, yet?"

"I don't know." Cara studied Ali. "On a good day, I could do it. On a bad one, I barely have the energy to crawl out of bed. What's your and Ram's experience with PTSD? Is a month too early after a trauma to go back to work?" She held Ali's somber gaze.

"Delos has hired a substitute teacher until you can come back, Cara. What I'd do if it feels right to you, is to start with half a day and see how you hold up. And on a bad day call in the substitute teacher. I'm sure Dilara Culver, the owner of Delos, will understand. She's been wonderful and caring. She has three adult children; all of them were in the military and all saw combat. She knows how PTSD can affect a person, and deals with it all the time in her own family."

"And that's why I think she was kind enough to send Ram out here to be my guard dog."

"Well," Ali said, "getting kidnapped in the middle of the city you were born in, in broad daylight, makes a person pretty jumpy. Dilara wants a personal security guy with you wherever you go for a while, even if you decide to bike or drive to school instead of walk. That security contractor will be with you at the school and during your commute to and from work."

"Which," she whispered, "looks so daunting to me, Ali. I'm afraid to walk outside that door. It's *loco*! It's just crazy. My mind knows better, but emotionally all I want to do is hide in a corner and cry at the thought of leaving the safety of Mama and Papa's home."

Reaching out, Ali touched Cara's small, delicate hand. "I know, and in time, those fears will recede and you'll push through them and get to where you want to go. It's something you need to overcome, and you're getting there, Cara. I see your progress every day."

"I thought about speaking to Ram about taking next steps, like trying to start going outside."

"I've got some news about Ram," Ali saw the opportunity to give Cara the latest news. "His boss needs him back in Alexandria in seven days, Cara." She held up her hand, seeing Cara's eyes widen with fear. "It's okay, don't worry." She added quickly, "He's sending a replacement contractor, a guy Ram and I both know, to take his place. His name is Tyler Hutton, and he'll be here with you." She saw Cara's face fall with disappointment.

"But," Cara stammered, "there's no one better than Ram. You've said so yourself. He makes me feel so safe," her voice thinned out and she looked away, brows drawing together.

Keeping her voice neutral, knowing this change would upset her sister, Ali said, "Ram is going to be sent Tyler's photo and résumé, and you can read through it and evaluate how you feel about him. If you don't feel there's a good vibe between you, Wyatt will pick someone else until you're completely satisfied with the replacement. Delos Charity wants you happy and feeling safe, Cara. They want you to heal up so that you can go back to what you love doing: teaching kindergarten children. What's most important here is that you feel comfortable with the operator who's guarding you. Okay?"

Instantly, she saw Cara's expression grow calmer. Ali knew that sudden changes to the status quo could seem like impossible challenges to overcome. But it couldn't be helped and she wanted to be the one to break the news to her. Ram had urged her outdoors on a number of occasions, working with her, helping her to gain her confidence. They got along well with one another. And Ali could see her sister idolized

Ram. He was so self-confident, quiet, and listened to her without interruption. All those traits had combined in Cara's mind to lean heavily on Ram. Now, he was going to have to leave.

She watched Cara begin to knit again, fingers trembling. How badly she wished she could help Cara, but this was something she was going to have to deal with alone. Soon enough, she'd be gone too, but Ali wasn't bringing that up to Cara today. Losing Ram was upsetting enough.

"How does Ram feel about this, Ali?"

"Honestly, he doesn't mind doing PSD work, but this is not his real job with Artemis. He's doing it because I asked him to be here with you. He was the one who led the rescue to get all of you out of that fortress."

Ali wasn't going to give herself any credit because what she did was top secret and her sister could never know the full extent of her involvement in getting her set free.

"Oh," she murmured, giving her a quick glance. "I guess he's a leader and he's probably feeling pretty antsy about getting back to doing what he loves to do."

"Not exactly," Ali countered. "He works with Wyatt Lockwood on creating missions to help other people in similar situations like yours. He's their Senior Analyst for Central America. There's a lot of activity with Delos Charities in that part of the world."

"So if others are in trouble, he's sent to free them, like he did for the four of us?"

Giving her a proud look, Ali nodded. "You catch on fast, Cara." It was the first time that she'd thought about others in that mission, showing Ali that she was coming out from beneath the worst of her shock. When a person started thinking about others, it was a good sign.

Cara managed a one-shouldered shrug. "I know you've never shared much about your military life because it was top secret. I'm sure Ram's is the same."

"It is."

"That was so nice of Ram to do this for me. I didn't realize any of this. He's really put himself out there for me."

"He's got a big heart," Ali agreed, loving her sister for trying to stretch beyond her own issues to see others and the responsibilities they carried. Cara had never been selfish. Just the opposite, and Ali was seeing more and more of her sister's old self come back every day, even if Cara didn't.

"Do you know how Ram looks at you when you aren't aware of it?" Cara asked suddenly.

Ali's eyes widened in surprise. "What are you talking about?"

Smiling coyly, Cara said, "You don't know, do you?"

Raising a brow, Ali held on to her impatience. "Know what? What do you see that I don't?" Cara was highly sensitive to her surroundings and always had been. She was good at reading body language, voice intonation, and was a facial expression translator with her kindergarten children. She used these abilities with great success when working with her young charges.

Ali had the same set of skills, probably through their mother's genes, because she was "scary psychic," but in her case, she used them in a very different environment to stay alive.

"When I'm in the living room, usually at night after dinner, and Mama and Papa are sitting and watching the news, you and Ram clean up the table and kitchen afterward for them. Sometimes," and she stopped knitting for a moment, "when you don't realize it, Ram looks at you. I've caught him doing it at least four times in the last two weeks."

"Looking at me how?" Ali demanded, frowning. She saw a small smile pull at Cara's lips.

"Like a man who loves a woman and wants her. That's the look I see in his eyes and for a split second, in his expression, and then it's gone."

Stunned, Ali blinked a couple of times, thinking she hadn't heard correctly. Normally, she was never at a loss for words, but she sure as hell was right now! Cara's eyes had lightened, dancing with amusement, and there was a mischievous look in her expression.

Moving uncomfortably, Ali muttered, "That's impossible."

"How many relationships have you had, Ali?"

"Not many. But what's that got to do with anything?"

"The look Ram sends you is that of a man yearning to give you some loving. I've had enough relationships to know that look when I see it."

"Well," Ali sputtered, "we're friends. That's all."

"Oh," Cara hummed, returning to her knitting, "that wasn't a 'friend' look he was giving you, sweet sister of mine."

Groaning, Ali stared at her for a long moment. "I've *never* seen that look coming from him, Cara. Not *ever.*"

"Maybe it's his secret, and he's waiting to share it with you when he thinks the time is right."

Shocked by her sister's observation, Ali jumped to her feet and went to the door, looking up and down the hall. Thank goodness Ram wasn't around to eavesdrop! She shut the door and leaned back against it, staring darkly at her sister who was giving her a smug look.

"We're just friends," she repeated. "That's all."

"Okay," Cara said airily, counting her purls on the row.

"This can't be," Ali muttered, folding her arms against her chest.

"Why not? When I first saw you two together I thought what a good-looking couple you made. Now, nearly a month later, I can see you have a very warm, intimate relationship with one another."

"It's *not* an affair, Cara. We're *just friends*. That's all."

"I believe you, Ali, but do you see how you're reacting to what I see so often? When a person gets overly dramatic about something it usually means there's some truth behind it. Come clean, huh? Do you like Ram? I mean, what's to dislike about him from a woman's point of view? He's pure eye candy and a great guy."

Groaning, Ali began to slowly pace around her sister's room, hands behind her back, head down, and her mind going into overdrive with her sister's observations. "He's a very good looking man," Ali admitted. "And loyal, brave, and responsible. You're right, there isn't much to dislike about him. He's a stand-up dude."

"And he's very kind to Mama and Papa. And to both of us. He's been here almost a month, Ali, and there's been enough time to see who he really is. Oh, I know he's guarding me . . . us . . . but there's a lot of time when he has nothing else to do. He helps Papa in the evenings and weekends, he's fixed things that have needed to be fixed around here for a long time. And look what he just did for Mama: giving her those under-the-cabinet lights in her kitchen that she's wanted for so long. If I was in your shoes, he would be a man I'd be looking at as husband material, nothing less."

A strangled sound came out of Ali and she pressed her hand against her throat. It was suddenly dry and parched. She walked over to the small table near where Cara sat. "I need a sip of water," she rasped, picking up the bottle.

"Drink away," Cara said, giving her a sympathetic look.

Ali drank deeply and then wiped her mouth with the back of her hand. "I'm just shocked, Cara, that's all. I mean . . . we just don't have that kind of relationship with one another. We never did."

"Maybe you're subconsciously working toward it and you don't know it, but he does," Cara ventured, looking up at her.

"I don't know," Ali muttered, upset, pushing her hand through her hair. "I've just never looked at Ram in that way. I worked as an operator with him in the past, before we went our separate ways three years ago, Cara. I never heard from him again until he launched the mission to rescue you and the other women a month ago."

"I don't know what to say," Cara said, knitting more slowly. "He looks at you with yearning. I see it in his eyes when you turn away from him."

"He's never made a pass at me, Cara, or even flirted. It's been a very professional relationship between us. Well, we are going to be doing something personal shortly. We're going for a horseback ride over in Cottonwood Canyon."

"Answer me something?" Cara said, meeting Ali's gaze.

"What?"

"What if Ram wants to change your connection with him? What if he sees you as someone he wants to have a serious relationship with? Someone that he liked as a friend, but perhaps he would like much more intimacy with you, now. People do change, you know."

Ali rolled her eyes. She wasn't about to tell Cara her deepest yearning for Ram because in her present state, her sister might accidentally let it slip to him and she wasn't ready to go there. Cara was her focus. Not her stilted love life, if she could even call it that.

"We're just friends. That's all, Cara. Nothing more." She hated lying to her sister, but it was necessary for everyone involved.

"You haven't had a man in your life for a long time that I know of," Cara pointed out. "Remember when we were little and loved playing house? We had our dollies that Mama made for us and played with them for years until the poor things eventually fell apart. Don't you sometimes want to settle down, Ali? You and I used to talk about who we might marry, how many kids we'd have." She sighed and gave her sister a soft smile. "Is that all forgotten now? Have you left your wish for a family behind you?"

"No . . . no I haven't, Cara. I guess I just haven't found the right man, yet."

"You're twenty-eight. Your biological clock is ticking."

"I know. It's not lost on me." She glanced toward the closed door. "Mama discreetly asks me about once a year if I miss not having children." She touched her belly. "I know what she's really asking: when am I going to settle down, get married, and have a brood of kids so they can become doting grandparents to all of them."

Giving her a wry look, Cara knitted another row on the red sweater. "Well, I get asked that question a lot more often than you do."

"That's because you still live at home, Cara." She saw her sister wince and then hastily added, "I mean . . . "

"I know what you meant, Ali. You've always seen me as weak, thinking that I still live at home because I need to lean on Mama and Papa for support. But you're wrong. I'm here because they need my help. They're moving into their sixties, and things that used to be easy for them aren't any more. I'm the one who is usually weeding Mama's garden throughout the week. I do all the laundry, clean the house, and keep things on track for them. Papa comes home at night and he's absolutely exhausted. He works outside in that awful heat all day long. Mama comes home from her job on the reservation utterly exhausted as well."

"Sorry," Ali muttered, sitting back down, giving Cara an apologetic look. "I didn't know all of this."

"How could you? You're never around, Ali. I don't mean to make you feel guilty, but your job in the military kept you out of country. And because everything you do is top secret, we can never have an honest conversation with you. We're cut off. I hate that I can't even send you an email. We've gone months without word from you. And Mama worries the most. It's really hard on her. I try to pick up the slack and help them with everyday stuff to make it a little easier for them."

Ali was stunned as her sister continued, wound up now and unable to stop.

"Would I like my own place? Yes. I make enough with Delos Charities, and I've saved my money for a down payment on a home. Mama and Papa won't let me touch my savings for them. Sure, I could have paid for an electrician to come out and put those cabinet lights in, Ali, but Mama wouldn't hear of it. She is fierce about me continuing to save my money for myself. She's tried to shoo me out of their house many times, but I won't go because now, as they age, they need my help."

"It's my turn to feel guilty," Ali muttered. "We rarely get to see one another anymore, Cara. And yes, I'm out of touch a lot. I offered to send them money home from what I made, but they refused it."

"I didn't know that."

"We need to talk a lot more often." Ali rubbed her hands down her thighs. "And getting a job where Ram works, at Artemis Security, is a done deal. My former boss in the SEALs asked me to come and interview for a position." She met Cara's interested gaze. She had quit knitting, leaning forward, all ears. "The job is a desk job, Cara. It means you can talk to me, email me any time you want, and I'll be able to answer you right away. I'll have decent hours, weekends off. I could fly home to Tucson some weekends. It would be a quick trip, but I could see a lot more of you, Mama, and Papa. I just didn't realize everything you were doing around here. I'm sorry I assumed wrongly."

Cara put her knitting aside and rose from the

rocking chair. She came over and sat on the edge of the bed with Ali. "That's just the best news I've had since Ram rescued us. Have you told Mama and Papa yet about this new job? That it will keep you in America?"

"It just happened a little while ago," Ali murmured, leaning against Cara. This was the old Cara she knew, not the one who had been so badly damaged by her kidnapping. Ali realized it was an "up" period for her, and she silently wished it would last for days. It would, eventually, but even a few hours of having her gentle, smiling sister back, who was so wise despite her age, was a blessing. It was nice to share this moment with Cara. Often, as children, they would sit beneath a tree, leaning against one another, talking about so many wild and fanciful things, and fantasizing about their futures.

Warmth filled Ali's heart and she lifted her arm, placing it around Cara's shoulders. Hugging her tightly, she said, "Both our lives are in chaos right now, but I'm so grateful that I have you while I'm going through it, Cara. You're my rock." Ali released her, and turned, smiling into her tender gaze. She saw huge tears well up in Cara's soulful brown eyes, and tears burned in her own.

How badly she wanted her sister back, knowing that this experience had forever changed Cara. There were things Ali didn't want to ever change between them, like their deep love and admiration of one another, their mutual respect and trust, and the loyalty they'd always shared.

Laughing a little, Cara whispered, "No. You're my rock, and our parents' rock, too! But I think you know that." She squeezed Ali. "You're my big sister. You take everything on for us: our home and our family, with such loyalty and responsibility. You've always been there for all of us when you could, Ali. I know we haven't gotten to see you much in the past several years, but we've all relied on you, anyway."

"Well," Ali whispered, blinking back her tears, "that's what a big sister is for. Didn't you know that?"

Giving her a playful shake of her shoulders, Cara said, "It's about time you met a wonderful man, fell in love, and gave me my first niece or nephew, Aliyana Montero."

Chuckling, Ali allowed her sister to give her a small shake. It felt so good to have the old Cara back! "You're such a dreamer! But you always were."

Sighing, Cara slid her a wicked look. "Dreams do come true. *Te adora*, I adore you, Ali. And I feel in my heart of hearts that Ram Torres is the perfect man for you in every way!"

CHAPTER 8

November 14

Tubac, AZ

RAM'S WHOLE BODY responded as he watched Ali's hips sway with the lazy walking gait of her palomino gelding, Luke. She rode in front of him. The two of them were following a sandy trail deep into Cottonwood Canyon. Ram's horse, a black gelding named Yoda, named after the Star Wars character, snorted, his nose almost touching Luke's white tail in front of him.

The mid-morning sun was warming the cool air on this late-fall day. The sun was bright, and the sky was so blue it would have hurt his eyes if he weren't wearing his aviator sunglasses and a baseball cap. He felt good, looking forward to this half day away from the Montero household. At last, he was alone with Ali. There would be no interruptions or crisis to ruin this special day.

He'd had a couple of days to feel his way through this upcoming experiment. Ram knew it was an important departure from what he and Ali had shared so far. He was a man of logic, not emotions, as Ali had always teased him. And in the month they'd been together for Cara's sake, something magical, something wonderful, was blossoming between them.

Last night, he'd snapped awake out of a torrid dream where he was actually making love to Ali. On the heels of a throbbing erection, he got up and took a cold shower. As he did, Ram had a startling awareness. Scrubbing a thick lather of soap across his body, getting rid of the sweat, he was finally able to grasp what was happening between them.

He'd had a month of living with a real family for the first time in his life. The one thing they had in common was their openness and vulnerability with one another. The more everyone in the family became fully available to Cara emotionally, the deeper the loving connection. And he had seen how well love worked as a healing force with her.

He turned that awareness around to look at himself and Ali. Damned if it wasn't the same thing happening between them! The first week they had been wary of one another, yet, they had cracked open that door between themselves and moved from antagonists to good friends who were building a relationship based upon mutual trust. During week two, they'd begun to open up a bit more, share with each other emotionally for the first time. And in the past two weeks, this organic 'thing' as he called it, had fed his heart and soul, made him happy and eager for more times alone with her. He wanted more of that happiness they fed one another. It was the most glorious discovery he'd ever made about himself with another human being. Stunned in the best of ways, Ram was looking at his life through another lens of reality now.

As he toweled off after the shower, rubbing his dark hair dry, another realization occurred to him. Whatever he felt for Ali was one of a kind. He was protective of her, even though she pooh-poohed his guard dog-like stance with her at times on past missions.

Ram had never experienced love as an adult but he was able to define and observe that mysterious emotion in constant, subtle action with the members of the Montero family. Not only did he feel a deep affection toward Ali, as well as surges of lust, he also found that pleasing her was a top priority. He loved to hear her laugh, to relieve her, whenever possible, of the burden of responsibilities that sometimes overwhelmed her. Whenever she looked at him with gratitude or affection, Ram felt as if the sun

were shining directly on him. And he wanted
more—much more.

He was still working through these feelings
as he and Ali clip-clopped along in the bottom of
the rectangular canyon. His heart and mind were
enchanted by having Ali all to himself. And best
of all, Ali wanted it as much as he did, from what
he could discern, even though they'd never talked
about it. Which meant that he needed to com-
municate with her as never before. It was always
a struggle for him, but he had to try.

Ram had noticed early on that Ali often
asked Cara a lot of questions when her sister was
under assault from her PTSD symptoms. Cara
would rally, perk up, and respond in a very
positive way to Ali's presence. That computed,
thought Ram. After all, questions got answers.
Questions showed care and concern. Questions
engaged two people.

Therefore, he needed to ask Ali a lot more
questions than ever before, so he could deter-
mine how she felt about him. What was she really
thinking and feeling? He thought he knew, but in
his new, tentative world that revolved around her,
questions were a good strategy for Ram to use.

He had come to another important discovery—it was time to open up about his past. The
more he shared, the less he'd have to ignore or
deflect her gentle probes about his childhood. He
didn't want to shut her out of any part of his life,

past or present.

Despite his fears of rejection, he knew he had to start revealing his past and hope that Ali would continue to respect and trust him. Ram held little hope of that happening. He was a kid without a set of parents. Four prostitutes had raised him off and on for the first ten years of his life. They were his mothers. He had no real father, and thus, no positive male image to show him how to become a secure, well-balanced guy. He'd been told all his growing up years that he wasn't important or integral to him.

His mouth tightened as they rode. Maybe, revealing a little of his past at a time wouldn't be so shocking to her and it wouldn't scare her away from him. In a sense, he suddenly realized he was trying to protect himself against what she might think of him. And he had to get beyond that point with her.

Ram felt inadequate for such a weighty task staring him in the face. The last month with her in the Montero abode had been a wonderful gift of living within a loving family. He'd never been happier or more fulfilled, and he knew Ali was responsible for it. The other family members had shown him a whole new world, a wonderful one, where they loved and supported one another. A new kind of hunger filled him, a yearning so strong that it dizzied him for a moment. If someone were to ask him right now what was the most important thing in his life, he'd have to say, "Ali."

"UGH," ALI GROANED with a satisfied smile, lying back on the blanket, hands behind her head. "I'm stuffed! Aren't you, Ram?" The shade of the green-bark Palo Verde tree kept her out of the November sun's rays, but also blocked the cooling breeze that came and went through the canyon. She watched through half-closed eyes as Ram put all the plastic containers away and stuffed them into the nearby saddlebags on Yoda.

"Yeah, I'm stuffed, too," he admitted, turning to meet her smile. He buckled the saddlebags closed and patted the horse's rump, then turned and walked back to the blanket where Ali lay like a satisfied cat on one end of it.

He sat down, about a foot away from her, pulling up one knee, his hands wrapping around it, the other leg stretched out parallel to where she lay on the blanket. "I've been waiting for a day like this, Ali."

"Oh?" She saw a lot of turmoil in his darkening green eyes. Always sensitive and aware of Ram, she could feel anxiety and worry around him. His dark brows drawing together, as if he were holding on to some deep secret he wanted to share with her, reinforced this sense. His expression was serious and somber. Something was clearly bothering him, so she sat up, crossing her legs, resting her arms on her knees, facing him. "What's wrong?"

"Nothing's wrong," he managed. "I've just been waiting for quiet, uninterrupted time with you." He gazed around the yellow ochre canyon, the walls about a hundred feet high on each side of it. "Personal time with you, I guess you'd call it."

Concerned, she said, "Okay . . . what do you want to talk about?"

"Well, I've been to this canyon before," he offered, gesturing toward where the horses stood grazing.

"You told me once you lived in Nogales, Mexico, and that's only twenty miles south of here. Did your parents bring you up here when you were a kid?" She saw him wince.

"A friend of mine, Mazzie, brought me up here for my ninth birthday," he began. "She was like a mother to me and she got a day off from work, drove across the border and brought me up here. In fact," he said, his voice growing hoarse, "it was near here that she brought a picnic basket and laid out a blanket, just like we're doing."

"So is this bringing back a lot of happy memories for you, Ram?" His frown disappeared as he reflected on her question.

"Yes, it was a good memory. Mazzie had made me a birthday cake and I didn't know it until she opened up the basket and set it on its platter on the blanket. She put nine yellow candles on top of it. Lucky for her, there was no breeze that day in this canyon and she used a lighter and lit the candles. I made a wish and blew them out."

"Oh, that's so sweet! Did she sing you 'Happy Birthday'?" Ram smiled, reliving the moment.

"Yes, she did."

Frowning, Ali said, "But I thought you had parents. You said Mazzie was like a mother to you. What did I miss, Ram?" Instantly, she sensed that he wanted to run away. Although he was sitting still, his hands tightened around his drawn up knee for a moment. Then, he forced himself to relax them.

"They weren't available," he admitted. "So Mazzie made sure I had a birthday. It was a nice afternoon being here with her. We talked and ate cake, and then she gave me a present that I wasn't expecting."

"She sounds like a wonderful person!" Ali said, although she couldn't understand why his parents weren't available. That made no sense unless they were out of the country or on a business trip.

"Mazzie was the kind of woman who truly cared for others. In fact, when I was six and having trouble in the first grade understanding English, she started teaching me to read, write and speak that language. Catholic nuns had taught her English starting at six years old. Until then, I only knew Spanish."

"Oh, no, that must have been awful for you," she murmured. "Your parents were Hispanic?"

"My father was," he admitted. "My mother was blonde, green eyed, and white. She was an American."

Frowning, she said, "Then, wasn't English spoken around you?" She tilted her head, studying him. "Were you dyslexic? Did you have trouble spelling and speaking?"

"No, my brain was fine. I was around only Spanish-speaking people growing up, Ali. Not much English was spoken."

"Oh. Your mother must have learned the language, then."

"Yes . . . she did."

Ali picked at a cotton strand sticking up from the old blanket that Ram had taken out of their garage. "But why would Mazzie be helping you? Why didn't your mother?"

"She was too busy, Ali. Mazzie really liked me, was available, and took a shine to me, I guess."

That didn't make sense to Ali, but she saw how uncomfortable Ram was getting with all her questions. She also sensed he was trying his best not to be evasive with her. So he was giving her a part of the story, but not the full story. Curiosity was eating her alive, but something warned her not to pursue this too intently. This was the first time he'd willingly engaged her about his childhood and she sensed she had to walk gently with him about it.

"You speak English now like it's your first language," she said, wanting to smooth away the tension. They were on a picnic and it was a day to relax and be in each other's presence. Ali had looked forward to this, so she didn't want to spoil it with her hundred-questions routine.

"Mazzie gave me a good, strong foundation in English, and once I caught on, it got easier. My grades started coming up and she pushed me to read a hundred English-language books a year. She worked with the librarian at my grade school in Nogales, who also helped. Mazzie was a smart woman and knew how to handle me and get me on track."

"You talk about her in past tense," Ali said.

"She was murdered two months after my birthday she had here in the canyon for me," he said, dropping the bombshell.

Ali looked shocked. What could she say to help him through this? Then, watching him closely, she replied softly, "I'm so sorry, Ram. She sounds like a kind of guardian angel."

"She was definitely one of the angels in my

life when I was little," he admitted, his voice heavy with grief and memories.

"So? That little puppy you rescued in J-bad? The one with the broken paw caught under a crate? You named her Mazzie."

"Yes. You asked me to name her and Mazzie's name came to me. I couldn't tell you who she was at that time. But she was a light in my life and always will be."

"I'm glad you had her care and support, Ram. She obviously made a real difference in your life."

He studied her. "You're making a difference in my life now, Ali." Releasing his hands around his knee, he crossed his legs, his hands resting on his thighs. "That's something I wanted to talk to you about. As far as I'm concerned, whatever is happening to us is good. I like discovering different aspects of each other that we never knew existed before."

She grinned. "I like it too, Ram. You're a different person here at our home."

"Part of it is your family," he admitted. "I'm understanding how a real family operates and presents itself to the world."

Digesting his statement, Ali knew better than to keep prodding Ram about his childhood. She'd seen him struggle to share something of that time in his life and she was grateful. It wasn't easy for him to open up, that she knew. "Well, I like how we're like two flower buds, each of us opening up, one petal at a time to one another," she teased him gently.

Nodding, he gave her an intense look. "I'm on completely new ground with you, Ali. I've often asked myself what I should do, or what I should say to you."

"I'm gathering you've never really had a serious relationship with a woman before, or lived with anyone?"

"Never. I had plenty of bed partners, but that's as far as it went. When we were in teams, I didn't have time to devote to a serious relationship. I didn't want to string women along, either."

"Most single SEALs are like roaming tom cats," Ali said, laughing a little. "It just comes with the territory."

He became serious again. "I don't know what to call what we have going on with us, Ali. Do you?"

A little startled by his question, she wondered at the innocence of it. Ram had had plenty of sexual partners when he was on her team. He never talked about them, unlike some of the other unmarried SEALs. Remembering her talk earlier with Cara, she offered, "We're learning to be friends, I thought?"

"Yes, we are. I haven't ever had a friend who was a woman before, though."

"Maybe that's why you asked your question?"

"I guess so." He rubbed his chest, frowning, and watching a red-tailed hawk fly overhead. "I don't see how you can be friends with a woman, though."

Laughing, Ali said wryly, "It's an interesting place to be with you, Ram. I've seen a few men and women who were genuine friends with one another, but in my experience, the friendship can often turn into something else down the road."

"What do you mean?" he asked, his gaze penetrating.

Ali wanted to tread lightly. Could Ram be that innocent about man-woman relationships? She was trying to cobble together the pieces he'd given her about his childhood. It sounded as if his real mother was indisposed, too busy, or maybe a corporate executive, not having much time for him. That would explain Mazzie being a pseudo-mother to him. Maybe she was his hired nanny? What she couldn't reconcile was that Ram didn't know English and it wasn't his real mother who'd helped him up and over that impediment. It had been Mazzie who helped him learn English. She wasn't getting a very clear picture of his American mother and Mexican father.

"I mean that I've seen a lot of men and women who started out as friends, and later on developed a deeper, more meaningful, intimate relationship with one another," Ali said. "My parents were friends for over a year until one day, my father admitted to my mother that he had fallen helplessly in love with her. He told her he wanted to change what they had so he could pursue her on a different basis. Of course, my mother had to agree to that or it wouldn't have worked. She later told my sister and me that she'd secretly fallen in love with my father about six months into their 'friendship.'" Smiling a little, she held Ram's intense gaze, feeling his full attention on what she was sharing with him. "Friendship is a great place to explore what you might or might not have with a person, Ram."

She decided that he was not very worldly when it came to a serious relationship. "Does that answer your original question?"

"Yes, it's helpful, but there's something more between us, Ali. I feel it here," and he touched his heart. "I know you feel something, too. But I can't speak for you. You have to tell me."

She became silent for a moment, running over several ways to answer that sticky question. Ali wasn't about to admit her torrid dreams of making love with Ram. No way. At least, not yet. "Well," she began hesitantly, "yes, I feel something good between us, Ram. I think it's too soon to call it anything but an extension of our growing friendship with one another."

"I've never felt what I feel for you, Aliyana."

Impacted, she heard the sudden thickening in

his voice, knowing his emotions had risen to the surface. For a split second, she saw Ram as a little boy, alone, with no one around him. Had he been socially stunted within his family while growing up? Did his parents not have time for him? Had he been neglected? Did his parents ever hug, kiss, or show they loved one another in front of him?

Ali believed the answer to all those questions was "no" from the way he was casting about asking such teenager type of questions. He was like a fish that had been tossed out of the water, flopping awkwardly on land, helpless. As confident, bold, and brazen as Ram was as a military leader, he was equally unsure of himself socially, especially with her. She could feel him grasping to understand, appearing to be on unstable ground with her because his questions were something a younger person, without experience, might ask.

"I feel our personal connection with one another is changing, Ram." She tried to think clearly about this because she knew he was hanging on every word she said. "I like what's happening between us. I enjoy our time together now, our private talks. I like laughing with you. I like seeing you smile because it makes me feel good inside when you do."

Ram sat there, digesting her words, taking them to heart. "I have plenty of friendships with guys, Ali. And while I enjoy being with them, when you walk into the garage where I'm working, my heart skips a beat. It's the oddest damned sensation. And when you laugh, this warm feeling flows through me, and I feel alive. So, I understand friendship, but what we have goes beyond that. Is there a word for where we are?"

Ali managed a wry grin. "I feel the same way about you, Ram. You affect me the same way when you come into a room. What to call it? How about 'growing closer together in an emotional sense'? Because that's what is happening to us. We're learning to trust one another, we're opening up. We are seeing more of the other one."

"It's nice," he rumbled.

"Very nice," Ali agreed.

"Does it bother you that Mazzie taught me English when I was young?"

Ali heard fear and hesitation behind in his question. "Why . . . er . . . no. Why should it?"

"You seemed, well, puzzled by it. As if it was an odd thing that happened to me."

Shrugging, she said, "I just wondered where your mother was, and why she didn't take you aside to help you learn English instead of Mazzie? That's what I don't understand."

"Maybe some other time, I can shed a little more light on the situation for you, okay?"

"I'd like that, Ram. I mean, you are who you

are today because of the way you were raised. We all are. You speak English like it's your first language, not a second one. So I know Mazzie was helpful to you in many ways, not just teaching you a language. Am I right?"

"Yes, you are." He slowly unwound and stood up. "I'm glad we came here today. It's brought good memories of Mazzie back to me. And I like our talks, Ali. Do you?"

She got up, brushing off the seat of her jeans. "I look forward to these private times with you, Ram. But that's coming to an end in about four days. Tyler arrives and then you take off two days later for Artemis." She came over, placing her hand on his upper arm. "I'm really going to miss you."

"But as friends? Can't we Skype? Talk on the phone? Stay in touch via email?" he asked.

Allowing her fingers to slide away from his warm, hard skin that glowed golden beneath the sunlight, she replied, "Absolutely."

"You're planning on staying three weeks with your family after I leave, right?"

"Yes. I want to make sure that Tyler and Cara get along. I want to gently break my leaving her so it doesn't impact her so much. I'm hoping that Tyler will make himself so indispensable to Cara that she won't even know I'm gone and miss me." and she laughed.

Ram smiled, picking up the blanket. He

shook it out. "And then you'll head back to the East Coast and be with me."

She took the folded blanket and placed it behind the cantle of her saddle, using leather strings to tie it into place. "I'm excited about the opportunity."

"I like that we'll be working together in the same section."

She heard wistfulness in his voice and turned, meeting his eyes as he lifted the reins over Yoda's head. Her heart tugged with so many feelings for Ram. "Well," she whispered, picking up Luke's reins, "I would love to work with you."

He stood there, settling the baseball cap on his head. "Maybe we could keep developing whatever it is that we have after that happens?"

"I never knew you to be such an optimist, Ram." Ali swung up into the saddle, turning Luke toward Yoda, seeing Ram give her a boyish grin as he mounted.

"If there's one thing I need you to know more than anything, Aliyana, it's that you've helped me to learn to hope again. That's a major gift you've given me, *mi princesa* . . . "

Ali felt as if Ram had reached out and invisibly caressed her cheek as he whispered that endearment. Heat crawled up into her cheeks. She saw his grin turn very male with yearning. Ram knew his roughened Spanish words had affected her and she liked it.

"I like being thought of as a princess," she said, moving up alongside him as they turned around to leave the canyon. Their feet brushed against one another from time to time and Ali absorbed Ram as a feast for her senses and heart. He seemed at peace with himself now and she wondered if it had been because he'd shared a little more about himself with her.

"Actually," he drawled, slanting an amused glance in her direction, "I always silently called you 'queen' when we were in teams but I never told you or anyone else."

"What? Was that supposed to be an insult, Torres? We were hardly on good terms with one another then."

"No," he said, becoming philosophical as their horses plodded side-by-side, "I did recognize you as queen of all that you surveyed. You came to us with a lot of hands-on sniper experience. You owned your turf, Ali. It wasn't arrogance. It was a bold confidence and we recognized you for who you were even if you *were* a woman." He flashed her a smile, baiting her.

Making a rude sound, Ali gave him a mock glare. "I'm sure you had all kinds of nicknames for me behind my back."

"No, we really didn't. It was tough adjusting to a female among us. We'd never had one before. But we never questioned your skills or abilities."

"Well, that's good to hear," she said, relieved. "I always had nightmares about you guys gossiping behind my back, calling me a 'bitch' and other such nice words."

"We didn't do that either," he said seriously. "First of all, Wyatt wouldn't stand for it. And second, we needed a sniper with us and there you were. It was the right place and time."

"I'm glad those days are over," she muttered, scowling. Glancing around the sandy floor of the canyon, she said, "I'm ready for a desk job, Ram. I really am. When you arrived at Artemis, were you ready to hang up your spurs, too?"

"Pretty much." He touched his left knee. "Arthritis is setting in and I want to keep my knees as long as I can so I won't need knee replacements. I'm trying to take better care of myself than I did in my younger years."

"So are you happy being in mission planning?"

"Very much so. Wyatt does send me out once every three or four months on a low-level mission, but that's about it. I asked for that just to keep my hand in things. Do you want to continue going out on missions once you get the job?"

"No. I'm done. Cara getting kidnapped, me having to sit in that tree hide and watch her and those women suffer, tore me up. I'm still emotionally gut shot over it, Ram." She saw concern come to his eyes, felt that invisible heat surrounding her like a warm, comforting blanket. She knew it was coming from him.

"That's what I thought," he rasped. Reaching out, he picked up her hand that was resting on her thigh, squeezed it gently, and then released it. "Even warriors get worn out. We're at the stage in our lives, whether we're in the military or not, when we look back and decide to make better decisions for ourselves now and in the future."

Her hand tingled wildly, pleasantly, with his roughened fingers sliding over hers in that unexpected caress. Oh! How she dreamed of kissing Ram again! His mouth was beautiful, strong, and well-shaped—perfect for her to trace with her own lips. Pushing those torrid thoughts aside, she said, "You know, I'm tired. I could use a rest. Looking back on it, I'm glad the CIA canned me. It was a gift in disguise." She saw a smile lurk at the corners of his generous mouth. "And you were an even greater gift to me when you came back here to be with Cara and make her feel safe."

"Do you mean that I'm a gift to you, too?" he teased.

She laughed. "Oh, you know you are, Torres. You've had too much experience with women not to know that."

Chuckling, he said, "Caught. And guilty. But I'm not sorry one bit, *mi princesa* . . . "

CHAPTER 9

November 20
Tucson, AZ

A LI'S HEART WAS heavy. Ram was leaving late
this afternoon for Artemis, and she felt as
though she was being torn in half. Could he have
become her second half, even at this stage? She
vividly remembered the kiss they'd shared during
the mission in Mexico. It was never far away
from her. She wanted to kiss him again—and
again.

As she puttered around in the kitchen after
breakfast, cleaning up the area, she heard Tyler
Hutton laughing with Cara out on the back
porch. There was a nice, large swing on it and
although the late-November temperature was in
the sixties, she'd seen Cara bundled up in a
colorful red, blue, and yellow sweater she'd
knitted for herself. She had been walking out the

back door with Tyler earlier.

At least that was going okay, and for that she was grateful. Her parents were at work, the house peaceful and quiet as she continued to wipe down the counter.

"Want some help?"

Turning, she saw Ram coming out of the hall from his bedroom. He'd been packing earlier after breakfast. How masculine and sexy he looked in a simple pair of jeans, a dark brown t-shirt stretched across that chest of his, and his sneakers. He worked out every day at a nearby gym for at least an hour.

"Thanks, but no, I'm almost done," she replied lightly, trying to hide her sadness at his departure.

He grunted, sauntering over to the coffee maker. "Want a cup? When you're finished, why don't you join me in the garage?"

She smiled. "Garage" was a code word for them now, their secret hideaway from everyone else, where they could truly talk openly with one another in private. "Sure," she said.

"Good. See you there."

"Okay." Her heart began a slow pound. Since their talk almost a week ago on their horseback ride and picnic in Cottonwood Canyon, their intimacy and openness with one another had grown in leaps and bounds. She was almost breathless with her desire to advance their relationship from friends to lovers.

She heard Ram leave with two cups of coffee in his hands and smiled a little to herself. He'd been incredibly thoughtful since his arrival at her parents' home five weeks ago. Every day, it seemed, Ram looked for little ways to show her he cared for her. And she knew it was more than just friendship blossoming between them now. The looks he sometimes gave her made her lower body burn with hunger. She'd not had sex in two years and whether he knew it or not, he was waging a campaign to get her into his bed, get inside her right where he knew she wanted him. Ram never flirted with her and she could see that he was trying to maintain certain decorum with her, giving her plenty of room to respond to him if she wanted to. And if she didn't, he never pushed on that boundary with her.

So far, Ali had not given him those kinds of signals, but sexual frustration was building rapidly within her. Even though her dreams were torrid, and she'd wake up in the middle of the night, aching to be in Ram's arms, she would lie there in her own sweat, her heart pounding, feeling trapped, unable to escape.

There was no way she was going to have sex with this man under her parents' roof. That just wasn't going to happen. She knew they would feel insulted, and she would never break her moral responsibility to her family with such a selfish act. Whatever was escalating between her and Ram was going to have to wait.

Hurrying to the garage, she saw Ram sitting on his stool at his workbench. As usual, her stool was standing a few feet away from his. She smiled at him as she quietly shut the door.

"I heard Cara laughing earlier," Ram said, nudging the coffee cup in her direction after she sat down.

"Yes, so did I. First time I've heard her laugh since she got home. What a great sound—I was so relieved!" Ali confided. She sipped the coffee and noted Ram's relaxed expression. There was something beneath one of his rags he used when he was working in the garage. It was pretty large and she wondered what it was.

"Do you think that's a good sign?" Ram wondered.

"I do. Tyler is fitting in with my parents and with Cara really well. He was always a nice dude, and that hasn't changed about him."

"Mmm, the medic personality," Ram agreed wryly, sipping his coffee. "I knew he'd be a good fit with your family, to tell you the truth. Tyler is one of those people who makes friends, not enemies."

"I believe you. Most men couldn't take Cara's ups and downs day in and day out. She can't help it, but it's wearing out everyone around her."

"She knows that," Ram said, "and that's why she stays alone in her bedroom so much. She hides to protect others from herself and those sudden moods that come over her." We know how gut wrenching they can be: scream or cry. Which is it?" He grimaced and shook his head.

"Well, we're a little guilty of that ourselves." Ali gave him a half smile, looking around the neatly kept garage. Since Ram had arrived, he'd cleaned up her father's messy garage, fixed everything that needed fixing, and organized the place so it looked brand new. He'd also done a lot of what Ali called "quiet work" inside and outside the house, and even helped her weed her mother's garden sometimes.

"Yeah, but we know when we're hitting that internal wall, that anxiety ramping up in us, the best thing we can do is go away for a while." He grinned. "Your father's garage has been a godsend for me. I've really enjoyed being with him, helping with some of the tasks he hasn't got time to get to. You're lucky to have him as a father."

"Well, Papa is so grateful to you, too, Ram. He works so hard at the farm and by the time he gets home at six, he's got no energy left over to come out here and clean things up. I know he's indebted to you."

"I'm glad I could do it for him." Ram held up his hands. "And I think I've fixed everything he wanted to do around here, but didn't have time for."

"Torres, you've done so much more than that for all of us. Most important, you gave Cara the stability she needed this first month since returning from her imprisonment. That's helped her more than anything to get on stronger footing. We're all appreciative."

"Cara's still afraid that the drug lord and his soldiers are going to come in here and drag her off to Mexico again," Ram confided.

"I know," Ali said sadly, frowning. "I'm hoping Tyler can help her remove that fear, and get her to start walking outside so she can start reclaiming her life. She told me last week that she really missed teaching kindergarten, and I feel that's a healthy sign. But she still has to have someone around who can keep guiding her and restoring her self-confidence so she can return to teaching."

"I bet Tyler will do it," Ram replied. "Look, he was a SEAL, Ali. You know how stubborn and enduring we are." He flashed her a warm look.

"You're right. You are all like that. But Cara doesn't know it."

"No, but Tyler is black ops so he'll figure Cara out, get under the armor plate she's got in place, and gently get her to go into a healthier direction. It'll take time, but he's a very patient man—umm, like me."

Her eyes gleamed. "Are you referring to me by any chance? Sounds like it!" Her lips twitched as she saw Ram's boyish grin appear. She loved these times with him since Cottonwood Canyon. His impulse to reveal some of his private feelings seemed to have triggered a bubbling intimacy that was just waiting to blossom between them.

"Caught. Again," he laughed. He set his cup down and picked up the rag that had been thrown over the object sitting on the workshop counter in front of him. "Here. This is a going-away gift I made for you. I'm sorry it's not wrapped in a pretty package, but I just got it finished last night." He set it down in front of her. "I guess the wrapping sort of symbolizes me, Ali. Plain and worn. But it doesn't take away from the gift I made for you. Okay?" He grew somber, searching her eyes.

Touched, she replied, "Ram, there's nothing plain or ordinary about you."

"Is that your opinion?" he prodded.

"Yes, it is." Ali felt her heart pound over the gift. "Can I open it?"

"Sure, go ahead. I hope you like it. I've been working on it ever since I arrived here."

Surprised, she tilted her head. "What! Out here in the garage?"

"Yeah," he chuckled, "away from your black-ops, prying eyes. It was the only place I could find that you wouldn't suddenly walk up to me and see what it was."

Laughing, she cupped the covered gift, placing it in front of her. "You didn't have to do this, Ram."

"I wanted to. Go ahead, take the cloth off it. See if you like it."

The gift beneath the cloth was about six inches high and almost twelve inches long. Ali had no idea what it was. "Okay," she said, giving him a tender look of thanks.

And then, she pulled the cloth away and gasped. Her eyes grew wide as she gazed upon a carved horse created out of slices of dried saguaro cactus ribs glued together with one another. "Oh, Ram!" she breathed as she delicately touched the horse standing on all four legs, its head lifted and tail swishing, looking at something in the distance. The ribs were all different colors, from wheat, to caramel, to white, depending upon the age of the wood that had dried long ago out on the Sonoran Desert surrounding them.

"This . . . this is so beautiful, Ram." Cupping the statue, she whispered, "You made this? Do you carve, too?" She saw his cheeks grow flush, as if her lavish praise was completely unexpected. That endeared Ram to her as nothing else ever would.

In some ways, he was so damned confident

and in other ways, completely unsure of himself.

"I've whittled wood since I was seven or eight. One of the cooks where I lived, an African-American named Joshua, taught me how to use a Buck Knife to create carvings." Ram gave the horse a fond look. "I spent a lot of time with Joshua in the kitchen. He was a gentle man with a huge, sparkling smile and his eyes always danced with light. I never forgot those things about him. He was a kind and caring man."

Stilling, Ali heard the deep emotion in Ram's low tone, saw more sadness in his eyes. "Are you still in touch with him?"

"No, he left his job as a cook when I was twelve. He was bringing a cart of food to the hotel, and a bunch of Mexican drug soldiers jumped him, took the cart, and then shot him. Luckily, he lived, but when he got out of the hospital, he left town and went back across the border to the US. I didn't blame him." Grimly, he held her shocked stare. "Nogales, Mexico, when I was growing up, was like Dodge City. Now, it's a war zone between rival drug cartels." Gesturing toward the horse, he said, "So, a lot of Joshua is in that carving. He taught me to use all kinds of wood."

Trying to pull herself out of her grief because clearly, Ram had lost a second person he loved, just as he'd lost Mazzie, she choked out, "These are saguaro ribs, aren't they?" She ran her fingers lightly across the sanded, polished, and then varnished wood. It was velvet to the touch, warm with life and Ram had made it just for her.

Ali was so overwhelmed with emotion that she needed to feel Ram close to her, to have his arms slide around her once again. He'd held her so tenderly when she'd sobbed that day, and she had never forgotten it.

She met his eyes and found there a blazing desire that was purely male, immediate, and powerful. She swallowed convulsively, her finger lightly tracing each of the horse's delicate, fine wooden legs. That beautiful, searching kiss he'd given her so long ago made her whole body burn with anticipation and need. It was tough to think right now, much less carry on a half-decent conversation with him.

"Yes, it is. Your father had a bunch of leftover ribs from making a tabletop over there." He pointed to the wall where they sat in a neat pile. "I asked him if I could use some of them and told him what I wanted to do. He was all for it and told me to take anything I needed."

"So Papa knew, huh?"

"Men can keep secrets too, you know." A sly grin edged his mouth as he held her gaze. "Do you like it, Ali?

"I love it!" she gushed, her voice suddenly quavering. "This means so much to me! I love horses. And this reminds me of our ride into

Cottonwood Canyon, our picnic together—good times, Ram. Thank you for this unbelievable gift." She pressed it gently against her heart. "I'll ALWAYS cherish this."

"Will you put it up on your shelf with your other horses?" he wondered.

"Better believe it! I'll put it in a special place where I can always see it."

"That's nice to know."

She grew sad, continuing to stroke the wood. "I'm going to miss you terribly, Ram."

"Yeah, I'm going to miss you just as much." He shrugged. "If all goes well, I'll pick you up at Reagan National Airport in three weeks. You'll sail through those employee interviews and find yourself with a job at Artemis alongside me."

"I know," she murmured, gazing adoringly at the beautifully carved, wooden horse. "This garage will never be the same for me ever again."

"How so?"

"I know I've always been sensitive about you being over-protective of me. But it was sure nice to have you wrap your arms around me and hold me when I needed to cry so badly that one day." Her voice lowered. "It was exactly what I needed, Ram. I never told you how I felt, and you needed to hear it from me. Your holding me made me feel better, feel hope again despite everything that was going on with Cara. You gave to me, you didn't take, Ram. It meant so much, you'll never know . . . " She gulped, feeling tears forming.

At that moment, Ali felt her life shift into a new direction and it startled her, but it didn't scare her. Ram was studying her with a poignant look and she swore he was embracing her right now, giving her comfort for their coming separation.

"I like what we have, Aliyana. I like hearing you think out loud, and then share how you really feel with me." He opened his hands, his voice growing gruff. "I knew you needed to cry so badly that day. You'd held those tears within you for far too long. I could feel you hurting. I guess I overcame my own fear of rejection by you because I was hurting for you in that moment. I wasn't at all sure what you'd do if I tried to hold you. I was terrified." He managed a half smile.

"But I went ahead and did it, anyway. I risked everything to help you, Ali, and you accepted my gesture." He shook his head, giving her a rueful look. "You're a powerful, competent woman and I know you can take care of yourself without me around. But my heart," and he touched his chest, "told me how deep your pain was, and I had to help you. That's the only way I can put it into words, so thank you for telling me this. It makes me stop questioning my actions toward you. The next time I ever feel that need to be held around you, I'm going to hold you—so get ready for it. If you push me away, I'll respect your decision. But if you don't, I'm going to hold you, give you whatever is left of my heart, and give you what you need. You are—and will always be—*mi princesa.*"

CHAPTER 10

November 20
Tucson, AZ

ALI PLACED THE carved horse up in the center of the second shelf above her bed, the place of honor. He was definitely her favorite. The best part was that Ram had signed his name on the horse's belly. She smiled at that, as if he had branded it and her at the same time. Unable to push away the allure of those dark-green eyes radiating his burning physical need for her, she'd felt shaky and unsure what to do next. No man had ever made her quiver with anticipation before—but Ram had.

Now, he was busy packing in his room, and she had closed the door to her bedroom, needing time to think clearly. She kept running over his story about how Joshua, a cook, had taught him to carve as a young boy. *Where the hell was his father? What was going on here?* His mother had seemingly abandoned or neglected him, and a woman named Mazzie had become his surrogate mother, instead. Joshua seemed to have replaced his missing father. And Ram had lived in a hotel growing up—what kind of family lives in a hotel?

She knew it was located in Nogales, Mexico, which was a border town and generally a very poor area. As a Tucson native, Ali had been in Nogales, Arizona and the sister city right across the border, Nogales, Mexico, often. While there were a few nice areas, the Mexican Nogales had turned into a city attracting hopeful illegals wanting to steal into the US. The coyotes who were willing to fleece these immigrants seeking freedom from Central and South American poverty took their money and dropped them in the Sonoran desert, leaving them to survive on their own meager resources. Many died of heat exposure and dehydration. And then there were those dark beings, the drug dealers, and the worst vermin of all who infested both cities like an epidemic.

She didn't even want to think that Ram's parents were part of some unlawful trade. Yet, they seemed to be AWOL from his life, and others who had genuinely loved him as a little boy had taken on the job of raising him, instead.

"*Dios*," she muttered, instantly wanting to reject that awful scenario. Ali didn't want to believe it. If she tapped into the pain of Ram as a little boy, abandoned by his parents at such an early age, it would explain why, when she worked with him on their team, he had behaved stiffly, like a robot. She'd been turned off by his lack of feelings, his insensitivity toward others, and his lack of self-awareness. He hadn't had a clue about how his actions impacted others around him—or so it seemed at the time. She'd been dead wrong about his capacity to be unselfish and sensitive to others. It just hadn't show up over in Afghanistan, is all.

Scowling, she looked up at the wooden horse. Her gut grew icy the more she thought about the bits and pieces Ram had given her the past few weeks. If he'd been abandoned, it would explain why he was still so shut down emotionally, and so distrustful of others in general. If her parents had abandoned her, she'd probably be a carbon copy of Ram. A child's tender, emotional being needed loving, nurturing parents and a safe place to give and receive affection. It seemed as though Ram had been given a terrible start in life, and the thought of what he'd endured almost made her ill.

Sitting on the edge of the bed, Ali rubbed her face, combating her feelings over losing Ram for at least three weeks, maybe longer. She had no idea how Cara was going to progress with her healing. She could be here in Tucson a lot longer than three weeks and she knew it. People suffering from PTSD had huge setbacks sometimes, for no reason at all. She knew her sister relied on her being here; it was an unspoken promise between them. Ali sat down and stared darkly at the brick-red floor tiles.

She was torn and miserable. How badly she wanted to ask Ram more questions and finally learn the whole story about his childhood. She wasn't privy to his personnel records where she might glean some insightful intel.

On the positive side, he was slowly opening up to her. Their budding personal relationship was based on mutual trust. Ali had never considered settling down with a man in her life until just recently, and Ram seemed like a good fit for her, and vice versa, which was a miracle in its own right. She had just never expected it to be Ram Torres.

Slowly rising, she heard Cara and Tyler talking out in the kitchen, their voices wafting down the long hall. She was unable to tell what they were discussing, but it sounded like a normal, everyday conversation. Cara wasn't crying, so that was a good sign. If only Tyler could become a beacon of hope for Cara, transfer himself into her life so that Ali could leave and get on with her own.

Her mother and father were also showing the strain of dealing with Cara's PTSD. Unlike Ali, she was unable to hide her razor-like, accelerating emotions. From the outside, Ali knew she looked "normal," and that no one suspected that she went through raging storms of anxiety, tearing her up and making her feel threatened everywhere she turned—just like Cara.

Ram had known, though. After reading Cara's debriefing report, he knew by just looking at Ali that she was ready to sob her heart out. That was the one event on his part that had changed their relationship forever: his unexpected act of humanity. Even more startling, he had comforted her and calmed her down. She had immediately responded to his ministrations, which surprised and relieved them both.

Ali's heart ached for his arms around her right now. She had never wanted to kiss a man more than she did Ram once again. To feel his reaction, to absorb his masculine strength against her, to soar with him, seemed like an impossible dream. Oh, but how she wanted it to come true!

RAM CUPPED HIS hand around Ali's elbow as they walked to her car. He'd already said his goodbyes to the Montero family this morning, and to Tyler. The early-afternoon November day was cloudy, with rain in the forecast. A Delos jet was flying into Davis-Monthan air field in an hour and Ali would drive him to the base so he could pick up his plane ride home.

He opened her side of the car for her, releasing her arm, and saw that she was pale beneath her golden skin. He appreciated that she was wearing her black hair down and loose, its silky tendrils dancing as the breeze lifted them now and then. He hungrily absorbed how she looked in the black wool trousers hugging her long, firm legs, and the bright-orange, lightweight wool tunic that fell halfway down her thighs. Cara had knitted that top for her a year ago, a Christmas gift for her sister. She was a stunning woman beneath the camel-colored raincoat that she wore over her outfit.

Closing her door, Ram walked around to the passenger-side door and slid in, pulling on his seatbelt. The car started up and Ali backed it out of the driveway as the first splatters of rain hit the windshield.

"Even the sky is weeping because you're leaving us, Ram," she said, turning on the wipers.

Ram reached over, pulling thick strands away from her cheek. "It's only temporary, Ali. You watch, the next three weeks will race by."

She pulled out onto the avenue, heading east toward the Air Force base. "I emailed Wyatt earlier and asked him to get Human Resources at Artemis to send me all the official forms to fill out. That way, I won't have to spend hours doing it when I arrive for the interviews." She already had the job. Now she was playing catch up with the paper trail to complete her new career with Artemis.

Brightening, Ram said, "Good tactic. There's enough paper to fill out to choke a horse." He saw her lips pull up slightly. Ali never wore makeup and he supposed that was because she'd been in the military for so long. One couldn't wear makeup, lipstick, or perfume when out on an op because the Taliban could smell it, recognize it as an American scent, and start firing. To Ram, Ali looked beautiful whatever she wore—or didn't wear.

"What will you be doing when you get back, Ram?"

"Wyatt has two new missions in Central America that he needs me to weigh in on. He sent the encrypted info to my laptop this morning and I've already started to work on them."

"Will you have to go on one of those missions?"

"No. I'll remain in the office."

"Good to hear."

"You know, in your new job, you'll be pretty much an office person yourself. You okay with that? You've been doing field work for nearly a decade now."

"I'm fine with it. I guess Cara was right: my biological clock is ticking and I'm not married and have no kids. I need to look at the whole of my life, not just live in a slice of it like I've been doing."

"Is that the Hispanic mantra I hear? Get married. And oh, by the way, give us a dozen grandchildren while you're at it?"

She grinned a little. "Mama and Papa are dying for some grandchildren and they've made no bones about it to Cara and me."

"Like every Hispanic family does," he agreed amiably. "They're family-centric. It's a good way to be."

"Have you ever thought of settling down, Ram? Having a family?"

Ordinarily, he would instantly close up on that question, but Ram realized that Ali's need to know was genuine. He tried to answer it honestly. "I love kids. All kids. But I worry about what kind of father I'd be, if that should ever happen. I don't think I'm good father material, anyway, and I worry about hurting my child or children. I'd never want to do that."

Frowning, Ali digested his unexpected reply. "But why would you think that you're not good father material?"

"The past," was all he said.

"It doesn't matter where you came from, Ram. What matters is that you try to be a compassionate, caring human being as you grow up and get older." She gave him a quick glance.

"You're certainly all of that now. I've been on the receiving end of your caring nature, and I think you'd make a terrific father if you gave yourself half a chance."

He sat back, watching the wiper blades pushing more and more rain off the windshield. "Funny. I never thought about being a father, Ali."

"Most people do, Ram."

"I guess because of my own past, I just never considered myself good parent material. I would never want to stunt a child's growth, make them afraid of me, or not be there when they needed to be comforted or held."

"You were there for me when I needed you here at my parents' home. And you were there for Cara. I guess I don't see you as you see yourself, Ram."

He decided to turn the tables, and asked, "What about you, Ali? Do you want to be a mother someday?"

She laughed. "Ask my parents? They're all for it."

"Of course. But what about you? What do you want or see yourself becoming as your life moves forward?"

She opened and closed her fingers around the steering wheel. "I've always wanted kids, Ram. I love them, as you well know. I was always up to my eyeballs with them at any Afghan village we visited."

"Yeah," he murmured. "And remind me, I want to show you something once we get to Ops."

"Okay," she murmured, perplexed.

Once at the Ops terminal, the Delos jet was scheduled to arrive in the next fifteen minutes, according to the flight desk. There was a light, misting rain outside the glass doors, and Ali walked over with Ram to a far wall. She saw him pull out his wallet. Leaning against the wall, she watched him, his demeanor serious as he opened it and dug into it. As he pulled out what looked like a very beat up looking photo, his eyes lightened, and his entire expression turned softer.

"Here, this is what I wanted to show you. It's a photo I took of you the first year you were on our team. When we rescued those Afghan children from the Taliban who were taking them across the Pakistan border to be sold as sex slaves. I know you didn't see me take this photo, and I didn't want you to know it, either." He handed it over to her.

Ali's lips parted as she held the small, well-worn photo up to see it clearly in the light. Its edges were soiled and frayed, with two corners bent, and she could tell the photo had spent a lot of time in his wallet. She was sitting on the back of the Unimog military truck holding Husna, her favorite child, just shortly after they rescued the fifteen of them from the Taliban.

Ram cleared his throat. "I . . . uh, kept this picture to remind me that you weren't the witch I made you out to be when you first came into our team. I felt a lot of walls around you, Ali, and I figured out it was because you were the only woman in an all-male team. But when you were with the kids in the villages, you changed so damned much that it just blew me away. I needed to get that photo of you to remind me you were a good person, that children loved you, and children are never wrong about who they can trust. That's why I think you'd make one hell of a mother. And any child you had would be the luckiest kid in the world."

Tears stung her eyes as she stared at it, the implications flowing through her. She looked up at him, her vision blurring for a moment. Then, she handed the old photo back. "I didn't know you'd taken this, Ram . . . "

He gently deposited the frayed photo back into his wallet and shoved it down into his rear pocket. "Even then, I was attracted to you, Ali, but I couldn't get past my own shit to appreciate you on so many important levels—not until now."

He looked away, searching for words. "Look, I know this relationship thing between us is new to both of us, but I don't want to leave here today without telling you how I really feel about you."

She wiped her eyes with trembling fingers. "What do you mean?" There was turmoil in Ram's eyes, in the harsh line of his mouth, the struggle she saw and felt around him. He bent his head toward hers so their conversation could remain private, his voice low.

"I don't know what to call what we have, except to say that you make me happier than I've ever been. When you come to Alexandria to pick up that job waiting for you at Artemis, all bets are off, Ali. I've had dreams about you since I met you years ago. That's why I kept that photo of you, even after your enlistment was up and you left the military.

"I didn't know where you went for those three years and I tried to find out, but I never could. Later, I learned that you were a CIA case officer out in Mexico and were undercover. That's why I couldn't locate you." He took a deep breath and then said, "But that didn't stop me from wanting to get together with you again and wave the white flag of surrender. I knew by looking at that picture that there was something damned good between us that had never been explored. There always had been something, but looking back on it now, we both had to grow up a lot in order to appreciate one another."

Stepping forward, he lifted his hand, cupping her cheek, nudging her chin upward so he could look into her wide, tear-filled eyes. "You make my heart smile, Aliyana. I wake up happy when I'm with you. I like our talks. I know I'm a mongrel dog in your life, but even mongrels can dream, can't they? I want a chance to know you a lot better. I want to open up to you, Ali. I want to let you see all of me. I'm not anything special, I know that. But whatever I am, it's all yours, and I will cherish the ground you walk on if you'll let me."

Stunned, her heart soaring, she stared into his eyes. Ram's black brows were drawn together, as if he were in pain. She closed her eyes, feeling the roughness of his calloused palm against her cheek. Pressing her cheek more deeply into his palm she wanted to burst into tears.

Ram had nothing to apologize for. Why had he used the word "mongrel" to describe himself? Who had called him that? Who had made him feel like an outcast without a family?

She felt her emotions bubble up until she was barely coherent. Ram was inches away from her, his body so strong and comforting against her own. She felt no threat, just that wonderful sense of protection coming from him and swirling around her.

"Tell me you want this as bad as I do, Aliyana. I have to hear what's in your head and heart before I step onto that plane."

Lifting her lashes, beaded with unshed tears,

she could no longer hold back the words. "Y-yes, I want the same thing, Ram. I do. I feel the same way about you."

Ali felt all the tension leave his body as his hand stilled on her shoulder, his fingers gripping her firmly, as if finally claiming her for his own.

CHAPTER 11

November 20
Washington, D.C.

R AM DESPERATELY WANTED to lean in those scant inches and kiss Ali until she melted into him. He saw raw yearning in her golden eyes. Finally, they were both on the same page with one another. *After all these years.*

"Mr. Torres," the man at the flight desk called, "your ride is here." He pointed out the window toward the tarmac.

Cursing silently, Ram moved his hand from Ali's cheek and looked in the direction the man at the desk was pointing. Outside was a white, Gulfstream jet with a simple nose to tail yellow and red stripe, signaling it was a Delos company jet.

"Be right there," he said. Turning, he saw Ali, now leaning against the wall, her hands clasped in front of her, watching him. So many feelings arose within him. He wanted to kiss her, hold her, and never let her go. None of that was possible now. He heard the baggage handler taking his equipment out the doors to the jet.

"I have to go," he said roughly. "It's the last thing I want to do right now." He dug into her softened golden gaze. "I'm as close as a Skype, as your cell phone, Aliyana. Call me. I need to stay in touch with you." *I need you*, he wanted to add, but the words never left his lips.

"Yes," she whispered unsteadily, forcing a slight smile. "I promise, I will. Get going, Ram. You have people's lives to save. I'll see you when I can."

Hesitating, he took a step back, reaching out, grazing her cheek. "Then hold this in your heart. *Eres mi todo*, you are my everything . . . "

He saw her lips part, saw the impact of his words meant only for her ears. Never had he seen Ali so vulnerable as in this unfulfilled moment. But he couldn't. Not here. Not now. And then, he saw Ali rally. It wasn't obvious, but he saw a glimmer come to her eyes as she studied him in that heavy, warm silence strung between them.

"I'll be in touch, Ram. That's a promise."

Nodding, he turned away. To stay would mean crushing her into his embrace, taking those lips of hers that he longed so much to kiss, melting her into him and becoming lost in the heat and ache of one another.

As he strode toward the opened doors that led out to the rainy tarmac where the Delos jet sat idling, he recalled Shakespeare's saying: *Parting is such sweet sorrow.* Now, he really understood what that meant.

As he cleared Ops, the light rain misting around him, wetting his face and the black nylon jacket he wore, Ram couldn't steady his feelings. How badly he wanted to turn around, race back into Ops and hold Ali. His mouth tightening, he hurried toward the opening where the co-pilot stood at the top of the stairs, waiting for him to board.

Somehow—and *Dios* only knew how—he wanted Ali to need him as much as he needed her. As he took the stairs, he nodded his thanks to the co-pilot, who then pressed a button and the stairs ground upward and folded back to lock the cabin securely once more.

Ram silently promised Ali he would kiss her again, and it would seal their future with one another. But he didn't know how or when it would happen. He didn't have a clue. Yet, something good and beautiful had been created by them in the time they'd had together at her parents' home. It was like he'd shed his old skin for a new one, learning how to wear it, feeling the room within it and getting comfortable because he wasn't the same man he'd been before.

He sat down in one of the dark-brown, leather seats and buckled his seatbelt. The Gulfstream was a working office for Delos missions and their people. He pulled out his laptop, placed it on the desk, plugged it in, and launched the Wi-Fi. The two missions he'd been working on earlier popped up on his screen.

He desperately needed something to distract him from leaving Ali behind. His heart felt detached from its life source, and he rubbed his chest as the whine of the engines on the Gulfstream increased. In no time, they were trundling down the ramp toward the takeoff position.

Looking up through the round window, he saw Ali standing outside the doors of Ops, watching his aircraft. Her arms were wrapped against herself. He knew that people who lived in desert regions got cold very easily in a November rain like this one. Her hair was a black cloak around her face and shoulders, making her look hauntingly beautiful and yet, so alone.

He lifted his hand, placing it against the window, hoping she could see it.

She did! Ali lifted her hand to him and smiled. His heart opened powerfully as he drowned in the sweetness of that moment.

Ram knew as a sniper, her vision was superior to most people, but he was surprised she'd been able to see him place his opened hand against the portal. Warmth and gratefulness, like heated ribbons of happiness, wound around his heart. As the Gulfstream turned away from Ops, he removed his hand from the window. It felt as if an invisible cord that was holding them together had dissolved in that moment.

Three weeks was a damned long time. He was going to bury himself in work to try and make it hurry by. All he wanted, all he could envision in his mind and heart, was picking Ali up at the Reagan National Airport and meeting her outside security. His dog Mazzie would love to see her once again—he honestly wasn't sure who would be more glad to see her—Mazzie or him.

Then, his imagination took over and a dozen scenarios played out in his mind, all of them with Ali in his arms, in his bed, and them loving each other, as they'd never loved before.

He was lousy with words but he knew he could show her how much she meant to him. Sometimes, touch communicated better than a thousand words, or a kiss, or . . .

Ram sighed and scowled, forcing himself to focus on the mission facing him now on the laptop screen.

A LITANY OF what she would say to Ram was

running through Ali's head as she walked through security, heading for the passage that would spill all passengers out into the main terminal at Reagan National Airport. She'd taken a commercial flight, business class, thanks to Artemis. They treated their employees as if they mattered, instead of stuffing them back into the cattle-car coach section of the plane where only misery, tiny seats, and sitting on top of your neighbor, reigned. Ali was grateful to have had Artemis pay for a business-class seat for her. It was unexpected, but a very nice surprise.

All she could really think of were Ram's last words to her before he left Tucson: *Eres mi todo, you are my everything . . .*

She went to sleep at night, lulled into heated dreams about them together at last. The next day, memories of his last moments with her before rushing off to board came back again and again. They tantalized her and softened the edges of her loneliness without Ram's larger-than-life presence. She saw Ram had wanted to kiss her. And she wanted to kiss him, but the last minute interruption ruined the moment. There had been no time left to simply come together and appreciate one another with a kiss that kept going on, and on, and on. How many nights had she dreamed of that very moment? Nearly every night.

Happily, Cara was doing okay. She'd had

some ups and downs after Ram left, but Tyler was adroitly situating himself as more than her PSD. The man knew psychology well and his Montana upbringing, his laid-back style, and that soft accent of his, served to calm Cara down, not hype her up. He was a release mechanism for her, even more than Ram had been. And that was good—very good. It left her not feeling guilty leaving her sister behind because Tyler was an angel in disguise to her as well as her family. He just had a knack for dissolving other people's tension, worry, and anxiety. She was more than grateful to him being in their lives when they needed it the most.

Tyler had cornered Ali at the end of the third week and been frank with her, urging her to leave. He reported that Cara and he had established a bond that should keep her stable after Ali left.

Ali knew the combat medic wouldn't lie to her. She felt some of her sense of responsibility lifting, and as she had packed yesterday for the journey east to Artemis, she felt lighter, more hopeful than she had in a long time. Ali knew it was because of Ram waiting for her, wanting to be an important part to her life.

As she carried her laptop briefcase on a strap across her shoulder, she walked quickly, wanting to get out of the herds of people, the noise and general cacophony that always drove her to distraction. Having PTSD just exacerbated her need to run away from all of the crowds and noise assault, to seek shelter, peace, and quiet.

Ram was that safe harbor for her. As Ali moved up through a narrowing hallway of the security area, she spotted him standing in back, a head taller than most of the expectant crowd surrounding the area. A smile pulled at her lips as their gazes met and locked. Lifting her hand, she saw him return her smile, and her need for him shot through her.

They had talked daily; usually in the evening after Ram had finished his eight to twelve hours a day at Artemis. She had never laughed so much, or felt so dizzy with joy, as when he'd share funny things that had happened at work. Sometimes it was about an operator, a mission, or some Texas slang that Wyatt, a real-life Texas cowboy and ex-SEAL, threw out during a mission briefing. Texas had a lot of colorful sayings!

Ram was usually the one person who hadn't heard the Texas slang before, and had to ask Wyatt what the hell he was talking about. That always brought a lighter moment to those briefings, often much needed. Ali was glad to see that Ram could take being the fall guy with good grace. He didn't have the usual male pride that made him resist admitting he didn't know something. More and more, she loved his humbleness and humility.

Today, Ali had chosen her clothes carefully. She wore a light-gray blazer, a tasteful, white silk blouse beneath it, and gray wool trousers. She had to look business-like for the coming day's events even though she'd already been hired.

It was barely eight a.m., and she was expected at Artemis HR at ten a.m. to begin a round of interviews. She knew there would be three, with Wyatt being the last one. Then, the assistant at Human Resources had told her yesterday, Wyatt would take her, Ram, and Wyatt's wife, Tal, to lunch at a nice little restaurant about ten miles away from the security company.

She was going to be busy! And all she wanted right now was to be with Ram somewhere quiet and private, with only the two of them.

But it wasn't going to happen. She swung out of security and saw Ram move to her right, walking around the crowd, heading toward her as she aimed for a nearby hallway that was less cluttered with people.

"Hey, stranger," Ram teased, moving off to one side between two storefronts, "welcome home."

Ali loved the deep tenor of his voice, the glint of burning need of her written clearly in his green eyes, that wonderfully shaped mouth of his curved in a warm smile—all for her.

"Thanks," she said, standing next to him, staying out of the way of passengers hurrying by. "You look even better in person, Torres. Did you know that?" She saw him preen beneath her compliment, his gaze intensifying as he held hers.

"Well, that's good to hear, *mi princesa*." He slid the laptop strap off her shoulder before she could react. "Let me carry this for you. How many bags do you have coming in the carousel?"

"Just two." She looked him up and down. The mid-December weather in Washington, D.C., was cold. There had been a snowstorm, the first of the year in the capital area, five days earlier. She saw snow banks outside along the wet, black asphalt roadways. Ram wore a purple sweater that Cara had knitted for him as a going-away gift. He looked damned sexy in those tight-fitting blue jeans and black motorcycle boots that were wet and gleaming from the snow.

The black, nylon down-filled coat that fell to his hips only accented his military-short, black hair and straight brows across green eyes that missed nothing. He looked like dessert to Ali. Should she tell him that? *No.* Maybe wait until all the official functions were done and over with at Artemis. Ram knew it was a done deal, and that they were only going through the motions this morning.

"Come on," he said, cupping her elbow, "follow me. I know this place like the back of my hand."

He protectively situated her on the inside of him, and Ali smiled at the gesture. "I'll bet you do."

"On ops we fly out of Joint Base Andrews. Here, when we have to take commercial flights, Reagan is our airport of choice."

"But you were picked up by a Delos jet three weeks ago at Davis-Monthan," Ali said, walking with him. He had cut his stride in half for her sake, which she appreciated.

"We use the Delos Gulfstream fleet when there's an emergency of some kind. They have big Gulfstream that can fly around the world, too. Dilara Culver, the President of Delos Charities, usually flies in one of them. She never flies commercial. Hates it. Can't say I blame her. I hate it, too."

"It's a pain in the ass to fly commercial anywhere anymore," Ali agreed.

He snorted. "Don't get me started." He took her down another hall, an escalator that disgorged them into the massive baggage claim area. All the time, he was looking around, always the operator on guard, always looking for what was out of place.

In no time, Ali had her luggage. Ram insisted on placing the strap of her laptop diagonally across his chest and claiming her two bags of luggage. All she had to do was follow him out to

the short-term parking lot. The street was salted
to melt the ice, the wind cutting, temperatures
below freezing.

Ali was glad to have the bright-red muffler
that Cara had knitted and gifted her with last
night, saying it was snowy and cold where she
was going. She'd pulled it out from beneath her
camel-colored coat that fell to her knees and
wrapped it warmly around her neck, tucking the
ends in beneath the front of her coat. Her long,
black hair was loose and free, like a warm cap
around her head.

Ram led her to a black SUV with darkly tint-
ed windows. He opened the passenger door for
her.

"Climb in. I'll take care of your luggage."

She nodded, more than happy to escape the
blustery winter winds. The sky had patches of
blue splotched between the dark-gray, low-
hanging clouds. The whole area was snow
covered, clean and pristine. Ram climbed in,
starting the vehicle.

"I'm such a desert rat," she said, laughing.
"This is damned cold weather, Torres."

"Yeah," he grunted, "I hear you. I have desert rat blood running in my veins, too. Now, I'm
going to take you directly to Artemis. The HR
team is there waiting for you. They're just going
through the motions, Ali. The most important
interview will be with Wyatt. He'll take you down

to the second floor below ground, beneath the farmhouse. He'll show you around Mission Planning. We all have offices on the third floor, with lots of windows and light, and you can see the world outdoors. But our planning sessions are done behind secure doors on that second floor. You'll get a feel for the place."

"Where are you going to be?"

He pulled out into the traffic, heading away from the airport on his way toward Alexandria. "First, I'm going to deliver your bags to another part of the third floor. We have a section for operators or people like you coming in to interview with us. They're like five-star hotel rooms. And then I'll join you later when you're with Wyatt."

"Oh, good, I'm glad you'll be there, Ram."

He threw her a teasing look. "Miss me? I sure missed you."

"Yes, I did. It was so good talking with you every night. That was a wonderful lifeline between us."

Nodding, he entered the freeway, the SUV picking up speed. "I'm having a helluva time keeping my hands off you."

"You think it isn't mutual, Torres?"

"Yeah, I think it is, Ms. Montero. I see that look in your eyes and that speaks volumes to me."

Chuckling, she sat back, relaxing. "First,

business."

"Yes, but after that lunch with the Culver family, me, and Wyatt at that nice little bed-and-breakfast place, it's my turn."

"What do you mean?"

"After lunch, they'll want you to relax. I told Wyatt yesterday that you were having dinner with me at my condo."

Her heart leaped. "Good move!" She saw the gleam in his eyes grow more intense. "I know you're a good cook. What are you making for us?"

"Are you open to a T-bone steak with all the fixings? I got some baked potatoes, sour cream, jalapeños, and jack cheese for them. Plus, I make a healthy salad. Oh, and I also made dessert—a chocolate cake because I know how much you love chocolate."

Ali reached out, touching his jacketed arm for a moment. "It sounds perfect, Ram. Thank you for doing all this for me."

"I thought, maybe after dinner, we'd spend a little time together. And of course, Mazzie isn't going to let you out of her sight. Later, I'll take you back to your room at Artemis. I'm sure you'll be whipped by that time. This is an intense, stressful day for you."

Shrugging, she said, "Stress was being in that tree hide watching Azarola's fortress. This is nothing in comparison, Ram. I think you know that."

"Yes, I do," he said, giving her a quick glance. "But I also know this is a different kind of stress. I know you're looking forward to starting your job with us. You have bills piling up and you don't want to take it out of your savings or put it onto your credit cards."

"You're right, it's a different kind of stress. What I'll really look forward to is being with you tonight. I've really missed you in all kinds of ways. After you left, I would go out into the garage and it would be silent, no one was there to meet me."

He chuckled. "Well, wait until I show you my place. And be prepared for Mazzie's adoring assault on you . . . "

CHAPTER 12

December 12
Alexandria, VA

A LI WAS GLAD to sit down and have lunch with everyone at the homey tavern along the two-lane road near Artemis. She enjoyed having Ram at her right elbow. To her left was Tal Culver-Lockwood. The Culver children ran the day-to-day business at Artemis. Tal overlooked the entire security company while Matt, one of the fraternal twins, ran KNR, kidnapping-and-ransom division. Alexa, the other twin, had run the sex-trafficking position, but later, moved to the Educational Division. They all had a lot of military experience and it showed in the way Artemis had been thoughtfully constructed. It was one of the most state-of-the-art security companies on the face of the earth, as far as Ali could tell. With Delos Charities giving it massive family financial backing, Artemis had the most advanced technology and equipment needed for black-ops missions. Money was no object for these families, who owned a hundred-billion dollar a year global shipping business.

Just before lunch, Ali had sat with Wyatt and Ram in one of the Mission Planning rooms on the second floor, buried deep within the earth. Wyatt had offered her two-hundred-twenty-five-thousand dollars a year, plus so many other perks. It left her stunned in the best of ways. And yes, she had accepted the job. Wyatt gave her a good ole boy Texas grin, rubbed his large hands together and welcomed her into the Artemis family—and it was a family, Ali realized.

For tomorrow, Wyatt had instructed Ram to help her lease or buy a home or condo. Two years earlier, she'd had a condo near CIA HQ, but had sold it because she was living in Sonora, Mexico. Now, it was house-hunting time again. Artemis had given her a surprisingly generous moving allowance, and what staggered Ali was that the company would pay for any lease or house that was purchased outright, so there was no mortgage on it. Instead, they would take a small, monthly stipend from her paycheck to pay Artemis back, without any interest.

Now, she understood why Ram enjoyed working with this dynamic group, who truly valued every person they employed.

It put her in awe of the good things this company did for its hard-working people. She was glad to leave after lunch and ride with Ram back to his condo in Alexandria. The sunshine was bright, the sky had cleared and was almost blindingly blue, with snow glittering beautifully on the ground, like a clean, white coverlet across the rural country road that led past the Artemis farmhouse.

She liked that the three-story farmhouse was a working farm with Artemis hidden inside. The farm had a huge, hydroponic operation, with many buildings near the house itself. There were farm employees who ran the multi-million-dollar hydroponics business. But once she stepped inside the farmhouse, it was actually a camouflage shell protecting Artemis from the prying eyes of the world, as well as from their enemies.

As Ram drove, Ali closed her eyes, feeling relaxed in his presence. He didn't try talking to her, seeming to understand she'd been bludgeoned with information coming at her from fifty different directions all morning. He sensed she needed some peace and quiet.

Once at the ten-story condo residence, Ali followed him to the underground elevator after they left his SUV in the parking garage. Ram was always alert and so was she. Being in black ops wasn't a cloak one wore and then removed; it permeated their entire way of life for the rest of their lives.

"My place probably looks pretty stark compared to your folks' home in Tucson," he warned her, opening the door and gesturing for her to go on in.

Ali walked into the airy, bright, multi-windowed condo. She stepped aside, allowing Ram to enter. "Industrial design style?"

He nodded, touching her arm. "It's got nothing on the warmth of your house," he agreed. "This way . . ."

They entered another area that had half of a partition separating it from the rest of the home. She noticed a black, leather couch, two chairs, and a nearby steel and glass coffee table. Everything was spare and stark, like an office.

To Ali, that wasn't what a home represented to her: safety, a nest to rest within, and comfort above all else. She missed seeing greenery. There were no living plants sitting in pots, anywhere. What did get her attention was that on the fireplace mantle there were two photos in frames. She recognized one as her SEAL team from years earlier. Another one was of her with Husna, the Afghan child. And that was it.

There were no family pictures, which left Ali feeling bad for Ram. Her parents' place had walls of photos of her and Cara growing up, and then, their later years as they all celebrated important events in their lives.

"I can see why you said this place was decorated differently than my parents' home."

Ram took off his coat and opened up a sliding closet door. He took hers as well and hung
them beside each other. "I'm no good at house
stuff, that's for sure," he admitted.

"Still," Ali said, turning, looking at the huge
kitchen with a gas stove, a big, granite island, and
steel stools around it, "I like the sunlight coming
through here. It really makes this place feel airy
and light."

"It's where I've landed between missions,"
he said, opening the fridge. "Would you like
some coffee? Tea?"

"Coffee sounds great," she said.

"Take a seat on one of those stools, and I'll
make us a pot while we catch up with one
another."

"Where's Mazzie?" she asked, looking
around.

"She's at a nearby doggie day care center. I
don't want to put her in a crate to not be able to
get exercise. There's a gal, Susan, who will be
bringing Mazzie home at six p.m. tonight. It's
only a block from where I live. That way, Mazzie
gets to go outdoors, play with other dogs and get
lots of love from the people who work there."

Still uncomfortable about the lack of human
warmth in this apartment, Ali sat down at the
island. The stools, in her opinion, needed nice,

soft, colorful cushions. She watched Ram work at the counter, his broad back to her. Down one hall, she spotted what was probably a bedroom.

"I warned you this place wasn't like yours," he said, setting a colorful, yellow mug in front of her.

"I don't think many guys know how to make a house a home," she said.

"You know, I felt strange coming back here after being with all of you out in Tucson. I realized the vast differences between your home and my place. Like night and day," he said, gazing around and scowling.

"Which did you like better?"

"Are you kidding? Your parents' home. It was lived in, it was alive, and it breathed happiness and peace."

"What do you do around here at night?" Ali wondered, looking around. The place was spotless, everything cleaned, dusted, and picked up, unlike her folks' home, or even her own bedroom. She wasn't messy, but her room had a lived-in look, while this place felt sterile. It reminded Ali of an operating room in a hospital: look, but don't touch.

"Usually I'm in my office." He pointed down the hall, "working with Wyatt's mission planning software for an upcoming op."

"Do you ever watch TV or movies?"

He grinned a little. "Not usually."

"Judging from the amount of work and number of missions that Wyatt showed me on that mission board, you're all way too busy."

"Delos has eighteen-hundred charities located around the world. There is KNR, kidnapping-and-ransom, attacks on one or more of those sites, theft of property and food, and a hundred other things that could go wrong at any one of them. And when it's reported to Delos HQ here in Alexandria, we're tasked with finding and fixing the problem, catching the bad guys, rescuing the woman or children who were kidnapped, etcetera."

"Matt Culver seems to be over his head in work."

"Yes, but he loves it that way. The guy hates standing still for more than thirty seconds. He's more than up to the task. So many countries now use KNR as a way to get money. It's a dangerous fad that's gathering steam globally. Tal was saying the other day when we were in a planning meeting that they were going to be hiring the bulk of new employees over the next six months for Matt's division. KNR cases are exploding, Ali."

He turned, seeing the coffee was ready. He picked up her mug, and walked over to fill it. "I wouldn't want to work in Matt's department. I prefer the planning of ops at a slower pace. That's what I'm good at."

"Yeah," Ali said, pulling the mug to her, "KNR isn't where I'm suited either."

"Wyatt knew that. But he oversees all missions, regardless of whose division it comes from."

"Does the guy ever sleep?" she grinned.

Ram sat down opposite her at the island, a bright-orange, ceramic mug filled with steaming coffee. "He and Tal are married, but I can't imagine their life together with all the demands of Artemis 24/7."

"I saw the way they looked at one another at the tavern, and they're very much in love," Ali said wistfully. "That's the glue that holds them and this company of theirs together."

Ram became pensive and slowly moved the mug of coffee around in his hands. "Which," he murmured, lifting his head and holding her gaze, "brings things back to us."

The silence lengthened.

"Ali, I was going to save what I want to say until after dinner tonight, or maybe not say anything at all, depending upon how tired you are."

She could feel a subtle tension moving through him, saw his skin tighten over his high cheekbones. "What were you going to say? I'm fine, I'm not tired, Ram. You know I like talking and sharing with you. It *gives* me energy. It doesn't take it away from me. And I hope it does the same for you."

She hoped her sincerity would help ease that uncomfortable feeling he was radiating. There was more than just tension with it. She could feel saw-like teeth ripping into him. It was a sensing, a knowing she had.

In her experience, any time something was important to Ram, the corners of his mouth tucked inward. She understood this reaction was that of a person trying to prepare himself for a coming blow. Yet, she hadn't said or done anything to trigger that kind of behavior. What was he afraid would happen?

"Whatever it is, Ram, it's okay. I'll sit and listen. I truly care about you and I don't like seeing you tied up the way you are right now. Did something happen to you that you didn't tell me about?"

Ali wasn't going to dodge whatever it was. For the longest time, she'd felt as if Ram was sitting on a lot of toxic secrets from his past. She sensed that he was afraid to share them with her, but she didn't know why.

"I've been wanting to tell you something for the last month. I didn't have the balls to do it at your house. I figured after you got here, I'd spill it." He looked at her, waiting for her reaction.

"This is important to you, Ram. I'm here for you like you were there for me after I read Cara's debrief report. Let me help you if I can," she offered, tilting her head and giving him a tender look.

"The reason I'm telling you this now, Ali, is that I don't want to hurt you. I know we're growing close to one another. It isn't stopping, it's getting more intense and if I don't tell you about my past, I'll be hiding something you need to know about me. I don't want you thinking I'm someone I'm not."

She frowned. What could this admission possibly be? In that moment, he looked like a scared child about to be hit by an angry parent. "Well," she struggled, "I like the man who is here with me now. Our pasts shaped us, but they don't define us, Ram."

"Yeah, well that's what I'm afraid to tell you. I know you look up to me and respect me. I never, ever want to disappoint you. But I live in a special hell, fear, really, because you don't know certain things about me."

"Then tell me, Ram." She reached across the island, her hand on his arm. "Let me be here for you."

"After you know my story, Aliyana, you may well want to walk out of this condo and away from me. Frankly, I wouldn't blame you. I'm not the hero you think I am."

Her mind snapped back to his comment about being a mongrel. *What the hell did that mean?* Her fingers tightened on his forearm and she felt the harnessed power of his flesh responding, tightening beneath the red sweater he wore.

"This has to do with your childhood, doesn't it?" She released him and straightened, seeing surprise come to his expression.

"Yes, it does."

There was wariness in his tone, something she'd never heard before. "There are things you've dropped hints about in the past to me, Ram." She opened her hands. "I'm going to share with you what I think and then you tell me if I'm wrong or not, OK? I'm a sniper, and one of my traits is being able to put tiny pieces of a puzzle together so I can see a larger pattern than most people."

"Yes, that's true of snipers," he agreed.

"Do you want to go first? Or do you want me to tell you what I think I see?" She didn't want to take away from this moment because he'd brought up the subject, and she didn't want to stop him from divulging whatever it was that bothered him so much.

"Right now, I'm feeling pretty cowardly and I wonder what you see. Share it with me first, okay? Then I can fill in the rest, maybe."

"You've never been a coward, Ram. Don't use that word to describe yourself. You're one of the most heroic people I've ever met, okay?" She couldn't keep the emotion out of her tone, almost growling at him.

"There's all kinds of cowardice, Ali, but go ahead. What have you put together?"

"That your mother and father weren't available to you. That Mazzie and the three other women you mentioned were surrogate mothers to you as a child. Joshua was a father figure who stepped in and gave you what you never received from your real father. The sense I get is that your parents abandoned you very early in your life, and fortunately, these special people picked up that responsibility, loved you, and shepherded you through your early years. You said you lived in a hotel, but what child lives in a hotel? I can't put that together or understand it." Her voice lowered as she saw his eyes grow cloudy with pain and recognition that she had so accurately pieced together his childhood.

"You're really good," he said thickly, "and I guess I knew that deep inside, Ali. I was born out-of-wedlock, my father owned a broken-down hotel in Nogales, Mexico. He was a pimp. He had thirty women working for him as prostitutes. My mother—an American—was one of them, and she became pregnant with me. She went across the border to birth me in the US hospital in Nogales, Arizona, so I could automatically be an American citizen. Later I found out she wanted to make sure I had dual citizenship as an American and Mexican. According to Mazzie, who was her best friend, she wanted nothing to do with me after I was born, so Mazzie took care of me from then on. There were three other prostitutes that helped her: Pilar from Guatemala, Sophie from El Salvador, and Renata from Honduras. My father wanted nothing to do with me, either. He always referred to me as a 'mongrel dog,' and would kick at me if he saw me anywhere near him."

Ali said nothing, feeling her heart drowning in pain for Ram. It was so hard for him to speak of this because he appeared to be tearing each word out of his body, each confession more painful than the previous one. "I can't even begin to imagine how that impacted you, Ram," she said softly, sharing his anguish.

"I did get care and love, Ali. Just not from my dysfunctional parents. When a jealous john murdered Mazzie shortly after my ninth birthday, my world became a lot harder. Pilar, Renata, and Sophie tried their best to take over, but my father was brutal to them. They had to have so many johns a day and earn him so much money. They wanted to take care of me, but it was never that often."

"Where did you go, then, Ram?"

"There was a small room in the back of the hotel, near the kitchen. I lived there. Joshua heard about Mazzie's death and tried to step in and be there for me like a father. He'd find me hiding in the closet. I slept in it because it was the only place I really felt safe." His voice thickened, "It was also where I could cry and no one would hear me . . . "

Wincing, Ali reached over, squeezing his forearm. "This is so much worse than I could have imagined, Ram. I'm so sorry . . . "

Shrugging, he pushed on. "The only reason I'm telling you this, Ali is because what I have with you is good, clean, and wonderful. That's what you give me. But you never knew the real me. You never knew why I would never discuss my parents or past with you or anyone else."

She released his arm. "I noticed on your fireplace mantle that there were no family photos there. I guess I should have put that together."

"No," Ram muttered, shaking his head. "You've got a lot on your plate right now, Ali. Don't fault yourself for missing that clue."

She sat there, staring at him. "How did you ever make it to eighteen, when you could leave that snake pit?"

"With the help of the people I just told you about. They saved me in a lot of ways, Ali. I carry a little of each of them in me to this day. They were kind, wonderful people and I believe their care saved my soul and stopped me from becoming like the uncaring, insensitive people my parents were."

"It explains to me why you were so guarded with all of us when I came to the SEAL team,

Ram." She softened her tone, wanting to sound conciliatory. "I couldn't figure out why you couldn't share anything emotional or family oriented with any of us. Now, I see why. When a baby is abandoned by his mother, he or she knows it. Just as sure as breathing air, you felt your mother's abandonment."

"I have no memory of her, Ali. My first memories were spotty from four years old, onward. Mazzie and the other women were always coming in and out of my life. I didn't even know who my mother was until after Mazzie was murdered. Joshua told me."

"You went through a horrible, emotional meat grinder. I've always seen you as a survivor, Ram. Now, knowing the rest of your story, I understand why you have such inner strength, resolve, and endurance. From your earliest times, you had to struggle to survive. Some part of your brain, heart, and soul knew you were in for a hard, hard life. *Dios*, Ram, my heart bleeds for you." She choked up, wiping her eyes with unsteady fingers.

"Don't feel sorry for me, Ali. I didn't tell you this to make you cry, dammit." His hands moved into fists as if stop a barrage of emotion erupting from within him. He forced them to relax. "I told you because I didn't want you blindsided by my past. If you like me, if you want to have whatever the hell we have to continue, you need to know the truth about me. I'm a nobody. I was born into the world unwanted. No one cared except the people I told you about. They gave me a chance and I ran with it."

"I-I know," Ali whispered. "That just makes you that much more special to me, Ram." Ali slid off the stool and came around, seeing the surprise in his face. Lifting her arms, she said, "Come here. I want to hold you. All I want to do is to hold you, Ram."

He made an inarticulate sound, turned toward her, opened his arms, and she walked into them, slid her hands around his broad shoulders, and pressed herself fully against him, her brow rested against the hard line of his jaw.

"You're so courageous—so unselfish, Ram," she whispered, closing her eyes, feeling his arms wrap around her slender body, pressing her tightly to him. "You're more than a survivor. Opening yourself up to me only makes me want you more, not less, Ram. Your story doesn't scare me off. It only makes me respect you more than I did before." Her arms tightened around him and she felt the tension begin to bleed out of him.

She heard Ram groan her name, his lips pressing against her hair, her temple, caressing her cheek so tenderly with his roughened fingertips that it made her tears fall. "Don't you *ever* refer to yourself as a 'mongrel dog' again, Ram Torres. I don't want to hear those words spoken again by you. Do you hear me?"

A rumble of laughter rolled up through his chest as he slid his fingers through her loose hair, leaning down, his moist breath flowing across her face.

"I hear you. Now, I want to kiss you, *mi princesa . . .*"

She closed her eyes, filling herself with his scent, his physicality, and his hard, unyielding body against her supple, curved, rounded one.

"*Mi cielo,* kiss me . . . " she whispered as his mouth eased lightly across hers with gentle invitation to kiss him in return—and Ali wanted nothing more than to do exactly that.

CHAPTER 13

R AM WAS SO hungry for this woman! He wanted to devour Ali's lips, her softness, and absorb her feminine strength. She pressed herself wantonly against him, eagerly glorying in his mouth on hers, letting him know she wanted much, much more of him.

Ram was dazed by Ali's acceptance of his childhood, as if it didn't matter. *How could that be?* Then, a small fragment of thought cut through the heat of Ali's mouth building mutually with his own. The reason he had made a big deal out of it was because the overwhelming message his parents had given him was that he was not wanted. But Ali wanted him, and he wanted her.

It didn't matter to her about his childhood except to break her heart as she heard how painful it had been for him. He'd been surprised by her tears, her trembling voice, the anguish in her eyes as he shared the story with her. She now slid her hands down his arms, feeling their hard, warm strength.

He moved his hands upward, framing her face, feeling her breasts pressed fully against his chest, and there was no question in Ram's mind or heart what she wanted.

"Aliyana . . . " he rasped, his voice off key as he eased away from her wet, full lips. "Wait . . . we need to talk . . . just a little bit?" He saw her thick, black lashes barely rise to reveal the gold in the depths of her light-brown eyes, and he recognized it for what it was: lust and sex. But going to bed with her? It was much, much more than that. "I want you. All of you. In my bed, inside you. I need to hear what you want, *mi tesoro*, my treasure."

Her lips lifted. "I want you, Ram, all of you. Any way I can have you. This has been coming for a long, long time and you know it."

His mouth widened into a grin. "That's true. Even when you were in our SEAL team, I wanted you. I never told you that, though." He slid his fingers through her black hair, hearing a purring sound in the back of her throat, her eyes closing momentarily as she responded to his stroking.

"Then," he rasped, caressing her warm, firm

cheek, "it's settled? We're going to bed with one another? Right now?"

If he had his way about it, Aliyana would never leave his bed again. That was how strongly he felt toward her. Joy infused him as her lashes lifted, amusement gleaming in her golden gaze.

"It's settled." She eased away just enough to move her hands against his upper chest, luxuriating in touching him, pleasing him in another way. "I'm on the pill. I don't have any health issues. What about you?"

"Same. Clean and no STDs. I'm good." He saw her smile deepen.

"Oh, I'm sure you're very good, Torres. I can't tell you how many nights I've had dreams of doing this, loving you, having you inside me where you belong."

Those words fired through him and he felt his heart fill with such happiness, he could barely breathe. He'd known Ali long enough to realize that what she said, she meant. "Shall I use a condom?"

"No," she said shaking her head. "Do you really want to wear one, Ram?"

"Not unless you want it."

"I don't want it." She broke his embrace and slid her hand into his. "Show me your bedroom."

"It's three hours before Mazzie arrives home. What about dinner?"

"It can wait. I'm always hungry after making

love."

He enjoyed her boldness. "Same here."

"We're more alike than you think."

"Let's go to bed and find out, eh?" He saw the gleam in her eye of the huntress that she really was. "I want to be stalked by you," he teased. The laughter in her eyes deepened, and she tossed her head, pulling him along.

"Never bedded a sniper before, huh, Torres?"

He slid his arm around her shoulders, drawing her against his side as they walked down the hall. "No, and I'm eager to find out if it'll be how I think it'll be."

"Be prepared," she warned, laughing.

He brought her into the darkened room, moving to the steel and wood dresser. On top of it was a small lamp. When he turned it on, it shed just enough light for them to see one another. "Is the light okay?" he asked.

"Mmmm, fine." Ali turned to him, placing her hands on his chest, giving him a playful look. "I like to see your expressions, Ram. I'm a super-sensitive person, so every touch, every sound, your scent, makes me ache for you."

Glorying in her boldness, he countered, "Come on, then, and get in bed with me. I want to slowly undress you, Aliyana. I want to get to know you, from the top of your head all the way down to your toes. What do you want?" He hoped it was the same thing.

"Slow loving is fine with me," she said softly, "but sometimes, I want it fast and hard, too."

"I can accommodate anything you want. All you have to do is tell me. I want to please you, hear your screams of pleasure . . . "

She climbed onto the large, king-sized bed. It was covered with a black, velvet bedspread. "I won't be the only one making sounds," she promised wickedly.

He joined her, kneeling in front of her, their knees touching lightly against one another. "That's music to my ears. I'm going to drown all of me—my heart, and soul, and body into yours, Aliyana." He slid his thick fingers through her luxuriant tresses, marveling in the pleasure on her face. Her hair felt like cool, strong silk as he moved the strands over her shoulders. He loved how relaxed she was with him, her hands on her curved thighs, allowing him to explore her.

"Oh," she whispered, opening her eyes, holding his gaze, "this is an equal opportunity playing field, Ram Torres." She reached out caressing the sides of his face, her fingers trailing down the thick column of his neck, outlining his shoulders, a pleased look in her eyes.

"Now, I'm being stalked," he said with a satisfied grin.

"Like it?" she asked, as she slid her hands beneath the red sweater at his waist, caressing his abs, feeling him tense and emit a low groan.

"I like it very much," he managed thickly, as she pulled off his sweater. She laid it aside, assessing his broad shoulders and the dark hair across his chest.

"Do you like what you see?" he asked, already knowing the answer.

"You know I do." She leaned upward, beginning a trail of slow, wet kisses from his neck downward.

Ram damn near came as she gave him sharp, little nips with her teeth, then soothed the area with the warmth of her tongue, kissing his tingling flesh. She held his upper arms captive within her hands and he knew nothing could make him move. This was pure heaven.

Savoring her warm, moist breath as she moved to his chest, continuing her nipping, licking, and kissing, he felt his erection harden in two heartbeats. Aliyana missed nothing, and he luxuriated in her stalking him sensually, making the ache in his balls intensify to the point of pain. He groaned as her lips captured his left nipple, teasing it unmercifully, and he growled, opening his eyes, a staggering bolt of heat jagging downward into his lower body. This woman was too hot to deal with and he gripped her upper arms, pulling her away from him.

"Keep this up," he said raggedly, "and I'll come in my pants. That's not where I want to come, Aliyana. I want to be inside you."

"We're on the same page," she grated, her breathing ragged. "Are you going to hold me like this or let me undress?"

Chuckling, he released her. "You're dangerous, Señorita Montero, but I like it . . . "

She quickly pulled off her clothes, dropping them on the floor near the bed. Ram liked the lacy black bra and bikini panties she wore. Black only emphasized the sheen of her golden skin. He quickly pulled off everything, watching her look of appreciation as she surveyed his thick, hard erection. She licked her lips, making a furnace of response surge through him. She was like an alpha, female wolf, getting ready to devour him in the most pleasurable of ways—but he was going to capture her first!

"You're mine," he growled, gripping her and turning her onto her back in the middle of the bed. He heard her breathy laughter, playfulness dancing in her eyes over his sudden maneuver. Pinning her wrists above her head, he nibbled at the hard peak beneath her lacy bra, feeling her suddenly tense, a low sound of gratification vibrating in her throat. Yes, he was going to please her until she orgasmed with him the moment he slid into her hot, tight body.

Savoring the other nipple, he felt her hips clash against his. He was taming her now! He smiled when she groaned, still holding her wrists with one large hand. Sliding his other hand beneath her back, he unfastened her bra, releasing her glorious, small golden breasts with rosy nipples. Aliyana was more than beautiful to him as he straddled her hips with his legs, his thighs holding her captive so she couldn't move. Releasing her wrists, he took the bra off.

"Now," he warned her gruffly, "those panties are next. Get ready . . . "

ALI COULDN'T REPLY, because suddenly Ram slid his legs down to capture hers, his calloused hands bracketing her hips, his lips licking along the band of her panties. It felt as if a fire had exploded deep within her. She'd gone two years without sex and she loved orgasms—how she'd missed them! But she knew Ram's skills would give her that mind-blowing gift. She arched upward, thrusting her pelvis, his fingers tugging the panties downward. For a moment, he got off her, just long enough to pull them off and drop them over the side of the bed. And then, just as swiftly, his thick, powerful legs moved between hers, spreading her thighs, opening her to him. His hands remained on her hips so that all she could do was enjoy what would come next. His tongue circled her belly button, lavished her rounded abdomen, heading straight for her aching lower body.

Closing her eyes, Ali gripped his thick, taut shoulders as he wreaked havoc upon her, licking her, nuzzling her with his lips, teasing her unmercifully, and fanning the ache at her swollen gate.

She wanted to plead with Ram to ease her throbbing pain, and just as she was about to, he seemed to have read her mind. The moment his fingers brushed her opening, a low sound came out of her. She was wet, a flood of thick fluid encircling his exploration as he stroked her, finding that wonderfully swollen knot, stroking it.

It felt as if her whole body had erupted like a simmering volcano, fire blazing in circlets and outward ripples as he urged the first orgasm out of her. It was almost painful in its explosive release because it had been so long since she'd had one. A cry tore out of her, and her breath became shallow, gasping. Ram knew how to prolong and tease an orgasm until it was truly finished and she rode against his fingers as they gave her such utter pleasure.

And then, his lips finding her hard, peaked nipples, he ravished them instead. The movement caught her off guard. She was still dazed by the orgasm's undulations and spasms surging down through her body. The white-hot pleasure of his teeth rasping teasingly against her sensitive nipples made her want him again. Groaning, she gripped his shoulders, using all her strength, pulling him upward, feeling his hard erection thrust against her.

"Get inside me!" she cried. "I need you now, Ram! NOW!" She heard a low rumble of agreement in his chest, more male, alpha wolf than human. He covered her with his large body, the warm hardness of him against the softer hills and valleys of her own. The moment he eased into her, filling her, stretching her as never before, she uttered a cry of relief combined with satisfaction. She arched upward against him, pulling him deeper into her, not caring if there was a momentary burning sensation as her tight walls began to expand to accommodate his unexpected girth and length.

It was a glorious sensation, one that she savored, aggressively thrusting upward, lunging against him, driving him deeper into her.

They both groaned, as Ali wouldn't settle for anything but all of Ram inside her, where he belonged. Even in her most torrid dreams of him over the years, the real sensations eclipsed anything she had imagined. He framed her face between his hands, looking down at her, his eyes slits, burning with need, wanting her, his hips thrusting in and out of her, establishing a pace that made her sigh and then smile. Her fingers opened and closed against his powerful biceps, hard and bulging, as he took her higher and higher. The sensations of silky strokes, his increased size, the pleasure he was bringing her deep within, brought her to a second, even more powerful orgasm than the first.

Ram continued to surge in and out of her, milking that orgasm until she felt as if she'd been hurled off the edge of a galaxy, tumbling end over end, wrapped in fire, the throbbing sensations and pleasure so keen that all she could do was sob his name again and again.

And then, just as she'd reached the zenith of pleasure, his whole body went taut and he released deeply within her, a low, vibrating groan tearing out of him. His hands tightened against her face as she felt him spilling hotly into her, creating a second wave of pleasure that made her lose her conscious mind. Wrapped in fire, riding an orgasm of pleasure so sharp and deep, Ali moaned. She had no idea how long it went on, but it felt like forever in the best of ways. To be wrapped in Ram's body, now protectively over hers, his hands cupping her face, his breath ragged against her cheek as he rested his sweaty brow against hers, satisfied her needs as a woman as never before.

As Ram eased out of her, drawing her beside him, Ali smiled weakly. She rested her head on his shoulder, opening her eyes, and gazing dazedly up into his. There was such gleaming pleasure and satisfaction in his eyes, and he was studying her with an intensity that made her heart open even more. His hand left the small of her back and he pushed several damp strands away from her cheek, brushing her flushed skin, leaning over and gently capturing her lips beneath his.

Ali had never been kissed as tenderly as in that moment. She was now drowning in a new desire—her heart's desire—as he cherished her mouth, worshiping her, adoring her. His other arm was wrapped around her shoulders, holding her against him. He needn't have done so—she had no desire to leave his side. Instead, she pressed herself languidly against him, letting him know how much she loved his searching, melding kiss. It said everything to her. She knew without a doubt that somewhere along the line, she'd fallen in love with him. And just the slick movement of his mouth cajoling hers, inviting her to return his kiss, told Ali that Ram loved her, too. She didn't care if he ever said those words to her because he had unveiled his heart to her right now. It was all she'd ever need. And at this moment, Ali knew this was the beginning of a new chapter in their lives, together. Once enemies, now lovers.

All she wanted to do was be with him, touch him, kiss him, and show him how much she loved him. In a while, their bodies would recover and come back online. And then, it would be her turn to show him just how much she adored him, how much she loved and admired him as a man.

There was so much more to Ram Torres than she had ever dreamed, and Ali silently made him a promise that by the time morning appeared on the horizon, Ram would know without a doubt that she loved him with everything she possessed.

Would it be enough? Would he want something more important in his life than just being in bed and having sex with her? Because Ali wanted forever. But what did Ram want?

CHAPTER 14

December 13
Alexandria, VA

ALI GROANED AS dawn slowly rose on the wintery horizon. The clock on the bed stand read eight a.m. The room was chilly, and Ram held her in his arms, pressed against her body beneath the cozy, warm covers. They hadn't gotten out of bed except for Ram to answer the door, take Mazzie, and bring her inside. Ali had gotten up, wrapped herself in his bathrobe, and walked out to the living room to greet the dog. Mazzie had leaped around, her tail wagging madly as she licked Ali's hands when she crouched to pet her.

Once Mazzie was fed, they left her out in the main living area where her doggy bed was located, and went back to bed. Around midnight, they'd gotten up and eaten a snack with Mazzie sitting next to them, expecting handouts.

Afterward, they'd come back to bed, their hands restless, and their bodies wanting more of the pleasure they had created and shared earlier. Exhausted, they finally fell asleep around three a.m., after their last, unforgettable lovemaking session.

She felt Ram's arms release her, and she tipped her head back on his shoulder, looking up into his drowsy, half-open eyes. She grinned and slid her fingers upward, nudging several strands of short hair off his unlined brow. He looked absolutely satisfied. The man was a stallion. He'd come three times last night. Three! That amazed Ali, but hey, she'd had a total of six orgasms in one night, a new record for her. They had explored and pleasured each other, and it was reflected now on their relaxed, tension-free faces.

"You look absolutely satiated," she laughed, feeling the prickle of his stubble beneath her fingertips. "Like an alpha wolf who's had his fill."

Grunting, he muttered, "I don't think we can do two days in a row like this, do you?"

"Wanna bet?"

He caressed her cheek. "All bets are off when it comes to you, *mi tesoro*. I've never been so well pleased." His smile suddenly disappeared, seriousness gleaming in his drowsy green eyes. "Thank you, Aliyana. Thank you for who you are, and for pleasing me more than any woman ever has. You're so incredibly special to me." He cupped her cheek, kissing her long and deeply.

Ali languished in his arms, drowning in the power of his mouth; the warmth and tenderness he shared with her that was so much a part of him. Already, she could feel his erection springing to life, pressing urgently against her belly. Slowly, their mouths separated and she sighed, opening her eyes, absorbing the joy radiating from his face. "All bets are off, Torres. You know that."

Chuckling, he released her and sat up, the covers pooling around his waist. He tucked her in to keep her warm from the chilliness in the room. "How about if I get up and make us coffee and breakfast? I'll get the condo warmed up, too."

"Good idea," she grumped. "I'm a Tucson desert rat and I can't handle this cold winter weather like you can."

"Hey, Nogales is in the desert, too," he laughed, playfully caressing her rump.

Ali gave him a feral look. "Keep that up and you're not leaving this bed."

"Oh," he crooned, moving his large palm around on her cheeks, "you've got a very nice ass, Ms. Montero. No question about it."

Snorting softly, Ali pulled herself into a sitting position, her black hair an ebony waterfall tumbling forward over her shoulders. "I don't think there's any part of me you don't like, Torres. I need a hot shower." She saw a gleam come to his eyes as she slid off the bed, the wooden floor cool to the soles of her feet. "Oh, no you don't. I'm sore. I need a break. We're not going to go at it in the shower. No way!"

He grinned and stood, stretching fitfully, his arms above his head. "Maybe another time?"

"Another time," she agreed, picking up all her clothes. "I didn't bring any clean clothes with me. They're back at the apartment in Artemis."

There was a dark-blue, terrycloth robe hanging off a hook behind the bedroom door. Ram walked over, picking it up and then helped her on with it. "There. Go get your shower." He patted her rear lovingly while leaning down to kiss her smiling mouth.

Ali had just gotten out of the shower when Ram knocked and cracked open the door, clouds of steam began to escape from the stall. "Coffee?" he asked.

Groaning, Ali pulled the towel around her body, tucking the end in between her breasts. "Oh . . . please . . . thank you."

Ram slipped in and shut the door. He handed her a bright-red ceramic mug filled with steaming coffee. In his other hand was a big, long-sleeved t-shirt and a pair of his white socks that he laid on the counter. "Clean clothes. Will these do for now until we can drive back to Artemis to get your luggage?"

She smiled her thanks and studied the white,

soft t-shirt shirt and white socks. "Yes, of course. They're huge . . . "

"I'm a growing boy, *mi tesoro.*" He smiled over at her, giving her a burning look of approval. "You're beautiful with wet hair and wrapped in nothing but that towel."

Sipping the coffee, she said, "That's a nice compliment. Are you cooking breakfast?"

"Yes. Bacon, scrambled eggs, and toast. With some chilies and good Mexican spices. Sound good?"

"Sure does," she said, placing the coffee on the counter. "Do you have a hair dryer?"

Ram leaned down and opened a drawer, handing it to her.

"About how long before you're ready to eat?"

"Thirty minutes."

"It will be ready."

RAM SAT AT the counter next to Ali as they hungrily gulped down their breakfast, no talking between them. Mazzie was giving them pleading looks and he gave her bits of her toast. They were more like a pair of mated wolves than human beings at this moment. He grinned to himself. He wasn't sure who was more starved from their night of gymnastics. Ali had dried her hair and tamed it into a ponytail at the back of her head. The white, long-sleeved t-shirt shirt hung on her, but she looked endearing and innocent in it. The white socks were big, the toes floppy, but she didn't complain.

Ram had baked some Pillsbury cinnamon rolls and put them into a basket, the scent of cinnamon filling the air. He laughed when she split the basket's contents, each of them getting four rolls each. Ali ate heavily, but given her job as a sniper, she burned ten thousand calories a day out on an op.

"I'm taking no prisoners," she warned him, a glint of amusement in her eyes as she eagerly bit into the first one.

"A woman after my own heart," Ram agreed, picking up one of his rolls. Just watching the way those full lips closed around that gooey, white frosted concoction made his lower body remember last night—and react accordingly.

Looking out the window in the living room, Ali saw huge white flakes twirling to the ground. "I love snow. It makes everything look so clean and white."

"Can you see yourself living here, then?"

"I'll adjust. I'm going to love my new job, Ram, and I think I'll be good at it. If I have to deal with four seasons, I'll do it."

"Do you feel up to looking for a place to live today, Ali? I know the area, and Artemis has a real estate company that works for its employees."

She licked her lips, her frosting-coated fingers, and then took a paper napkin, wiping them off. "I have something serious to talk to you about first, Ram."

Frowning, he said, "Sure. What is it?" His gut automatically clenched when Ali became deadly serious. He was afraid of what she might say.

"Us. You and me. I had over a month with you at Mama and Papa's house. You got along well with everyone. You were never a pain in the ass."

He smiled a little. "No, I had the garage and my carvings to make. I know that people need space, Ali. I gave it to them, and took some for myself."

She turned around on the stool, hands wrapping around the seat between her legs, studying him. "What if I told you that I want to live with you? To explore what we have or don't have?"

Stunned, Ram sat there, almost paralyzed by the unexpected questions. "Really?"

"Look," Ali rushed on, lifting her hands, "I know it's too soon . . . "

"No . . . no! It isn't too soon . . . " he countered. *Was this possible?*

She studied him, the silence thickening between them. "Then what's on your mind?"

"I've been thinking a lot about us, too, Ali,"

he admitted quietly. "I've had dreams—crazy dreams—that I thought would never come true."

"Tell me about them, Ram."

"I thought that you and I could find some-place around here to live together. I don't like this condo. I know it's not a home. It's just a shell. I want a home like your parents have. Then, maybe we could buy one and see if our relation-ship would work out, or if we got under each other's skin, instead. We got along fine at your parents' home." He studied his sterile, industrial condo. "I know this isn't your style of living. You wouldn't be happy here. You like trees, bushes, flowers, and a garden to weed, just like your mother does."

Her lips curved. "You pegged me on that one."

"Well, would you like to try it? We could go looking for a rental or buy a house with some land to it so you could put in a garden. I'm okay with that. I can live anywhere." And then he added, "I started out at a hotel, so a house like your parents have, to me, is like a warm nest—a real home."

Ram saw sadness come to Ali's eyes, and immediately said, "I didn't mean to make you feel sorry for me."

She reached out, trailing her fingers along the hard line of his jaw. "No, that wasn't it, Ram. I feel sad because you missed so much as a child, and yes, I saw that you truly enjoyed being at my parents' home. You relaxed like I've never seen you do before." She slipped her hand around his. "Now that I know your story, I understand what it meant for you to be with us for those five weeks."

He squeezed her fingers. "It showed me what heaven looks like, Ali. What I'd missed . . . " He drew in a ragged breath, expelled it, adding thickly, "it showed me that I could dream of having a house like that with you someday." He held her gaze for a moment.

She felt such tenderness toward him that her face flushed with feeling as she digested the full implications of his words.

"I will never lie to you, Ali. In my heart of hearts, I want us to find a house we can buy. I have more than enough money saved for one. I want you in it with me—and Mazzie, too. I want to live my life with you in any way that you and I see it happening."

Tugging gently on her hand, Ram pulled her off the stool and guided her between his legs. The softness in her mouth, the way she twined her arms around his neck, leaning languidly against him, gave him the courage to go on. "Ali, I had no idea what love was until I got to your parents' home. There, I discovered love between a man and a woman. I saw love between two sisters. It's a house built on love and I felt like a greedy beggar being there, feeling it, needing it, so hungry for what you were all sharing with one another. And when your mother hugged me, I wondered if you two sisters had felt what I did when she wrapped her arms you."

Nuzzling his jaw, Ali sighed and tightened her embrace for a moment. "Now I understand some of those looks that came over you. You were living vicariously through all of us, feeling so enriched and happy to be a part of us. You were treated like a very loved son by my parents. It had to feel so good to you!"

"It did. But I felt guilty, too, because I felt I was always taking, watching, and receiving from all of you and I gave nothing in return."

"Oh, but you did, in so many ways," she protested, leaning back, holding his shadowed gaze. "You contributed to all of us, Ram, whether you knew it or not. Especially to Cara. I know she wouldn't be as far along as she is now if you hadn't been there. You underestimated your worth to all of us."

Shrugging, he said, "I don't have much practice at this, Ali." He searched her eyes, moving his hands gently across her shoulders. "I want to live with you. Buy a house, whatever you like," he said.

"I've hidden a lot of dreams of my own from you, Ram," she began in a low tone. "I've dreamed of us living together for a lot longer than you realize. I just never could see how it could come about."

He caressed her hips. "Do you see it now, *mi tesoro*?"

Nodding, Ali rested her brow against his, eyes closed. "Last night . . . oh, Ram, last night was incredible. I had dreams of us making love so often over the years. Even when you were out of my life those three years, I'd still have those dreams."

He placed his finger beneath her chin and eased away enough to study her opening eyes. "And what will you do, I wonder, when I tell you that as early as the first year when you came to our SEAL team, I was dreaming of making love to you?" He saw shock register. And then, mirth danced in her eyes. Gently pushing dark strands away from her one ear, he teased, "I've wanted a relationship with you for some time, Aliyana. Now you know the whole truth of how long that dream has been growing inside me."

Sliding her hands down his thick biceps, resting her fingers across his forearms, she whispered, "It was the same for me, Ram. As much as we bickered, sniped, and got into each other's faces, I'd have dreams later of making love with you. It was crazy and I didn't understand it then. But I think I do now." She grazed his cheek with her fingertips. "I believe," she began haltingly, "that we fell in love with one

another back then. But because of your upbringing, you didn't know how to emotionally connect
with me. I believe you were just as powerfully
drawn to me as I was to you, Ram. But we were
in a SEAL team where we didn't dare fraternize.
Plus, you had your past to overcome."

Nodding, he said, "I've been thinking the
same thing, Aliyana. Chief Lockwood once
landed on me with both feet after you and I had a
row. He got in my face in the privacy of his office
and said he thought we loved each other, but
were too stubborn to realize it. So we fought,
instead."

"Did Wyatt know of your past history?"

"Yeah, he did. It's in my personnel file. The
FBI uncovered it all while checking me out for a
top-secret clearance when I went into the
SEALs."

"Maybe Wyatt understood then," Ali whispered. She sighed, giving him a thoughtful look.
"And he was in no position to undo the damage
done to you. We were a SEAL team. We had ops
to perform. We couldn't allow petty, personal
differences to interfere. We could have gotten
someone killed. Out on a mission we were all
professional."

"I often thought that, too," Ram admitted,
"but I never went to him about it because we
were a team. We had other fish to fry and focus
on."

"You're right. It's so sad, though." She leaned over, brushing a kiss on his cheek. "At least the truth is out in the open now, Ram." Ali stared at him. "Yes, let's go house hunting today. I don't want a rental. I want to buy. I'd love to find a small, cozy house with some property, a place where I could put in a garden and raise our own vegetables. Gardening is like meditation to me, Ram."

"I know it is. I would stand where you couldn't see me and watch you out there, weeding the rows on your mother's garden. I saw how at peace you were." He smiled a little. "How happy you were and I ached to give you that same kind of happiness, Aliyana. Let's go visit the Artemis realtor and find some house listings, then maybe go out and see two or three houses this afternoon. How does that sound?"

Whispering his name, Ali kissed him with everything she felt in her heart for Ram. "Like a dream come true."

He eased her away from him and stood up. "Let's get the dishes done and then we'll drive to Artemis. I don't want to waste one minute of this day on finding a house that we can make into our very own nest."

CHAPTER 15

December 23
Alexandria, VA

"WHAT DO YOU think?" Ram asked Ali as they stood in a two-story house just outside the city limits of Alexandria. He had his arm around her shoulders and she was leaning casually against him, her arm wrapped around his waist.

"I love it, Ram. It's small but cozy." She lifted her chin, gazing up at him. "How do you feel about it?"

"It's sure different from the glass and metal condo I've been living in," he admitted. This was a twenty-five-year-old Craftsman-style home, and he appreciated the hickory wooden floors, the curves above the kitchen and living room entrances, as well as the wooden stairs that led up to the bedrooms.

"Think you could live here with me?"

"I could live anywhere with you, Aliyana. I'm more concerned that you like it. I never had a real home, so this place doesn't call to me like it does to you." He squeezed her. "If you like it, we'll put in an offer."

She sighed. "It's like a beautiful, quaint nest. I also like that there's a mother-in-law house in the back. It has two acres, and it's fenced for Mazzie so she can really run around as much as she wants." She gestured toward the house. "There's already a huge, garden plot just begging to be planted next spring."

Nodding, he walked back with her into the kitchen. The owners had built the house. The man had been a cabinetmaker, and the hickory cabinets with their shiny copper knobs show-cased the true depth of his skills. "I really like the five-hundred square foot guesthouse out back as well. It's a place where your parents, Cara, or whoever else you wanted, could come for a visit."

"They'd love this place," she murmured. Turning, she left his side and went over to the expensive, professional-chef Wolf stove, check-ing it out more closely, opening the oven door. "What I like is that the man who built this did it out of his love for his wife. He was so skilled. And she loved gardening and growing things. I think it's perfect for us, Ram." She noted that the oven was clean and closed the door. She leaned against the caramel, black, and cream swirls throughout the granite counter and turned toward Ram, who stood there, gazing at the beautifully crafted cabinets in an L-shape around the large, roomy kitchen.

"Too bad the couple died," Ram said. "They lived here for twenty-five years. It's kind of sad."

"We're all going to die someday," she said somberly. "But at least they lived in a house he made with his own hands and heart. I'm sure his wife had a say in him building that guesthouse and creating the small fruit-tree orchard they have beyond the garden area. Their love of this place is a testament to them and we'll cherish it as much as they did."

"It was a teamwork kind of thing," Ram agreed. He gazed over at the long, wide island of granite that complemented the hickory cabinets. The floor was ceramic tile, a pale-apricot color that gave the kitchen a warm, light ambiance.

"I could be happy here," Ali said, running her fingers across the smooth granite countertop. "Could you, Ram?"

He smiled a little. "I'm just happy to be with you, Aliyana. I need nothing more than that. Maybe someday I'll feel like you do about looking at a home as a nest, much like your parents' home. A safe place, a happy place."

She nodded and caught his hand, leading him into the open-concept living room. "We've got a blank canvas in here, Ram. I can see we'll be spending money on furniture."

"Choose whatever you want."

"I'm going to drag you along, Torres. You are going to get involved in this process. A house is a home, not just a place to land and take off from. And it has to reflect BOTH of us. Not just me."

"Now you're growling at me, Ms. Montero."

She laughed, walking with him to the stairs. "Indeed I am. I need to tame you into becoming a nester like me and my parents."

"I don't think it's going to be difficult for me to make that adjustment. Didn't I quietly fit into your folks' home for five weeks without a fuss?"

"Yes, you did. I think if we're able to buy this home and get it decorated as we like, this place will grow on you like a good friend. And then you'll always look forward to coming home after work."

He brought Ali into his arms, moving his hands along her shoulders as he stared down into her shining golden eyes. "You are my home, *mi tesoro*. You are all I will ever need. Where we live doesn't matter to me, and probably never will, but I'm open to change. I was very happy to spend time in your father's garage."

"Yes, and this place has a huge, unattached three-car garage," Ali pointed out, lifting up on her toes and giving him a quick kiss. "You can have your wood sculpture shop out there. And our two cars will fit nicely in there, as well. I feel this place is ideal for us, Ram."

"It really is," he replied, sliding his hand over the crown of her head, fingers moving through the cool silkiness of her loose hair that fell like an ebony cape around the dark-green sweater she wore.

"We have to call the Artemis realtor," she said. "We also have the Culver Christmas dinner party tonight with all their Turkish and Greek relatives at their home in Alexandria, so we need to get cleaned up, shower, and get ready for that. Dilara wants us there at eight p.m."

"Yes," Ram said, leading her toward the front door, "Wyatt was telling me that it's a special invitation, and most employees aren't invited to their family gathering. But you are."

"*We* are," Ali stressed. "Dilara loves you. I'm finding out you're a favorite of hers—and she does have favorites, you know. You can always tell because she goes around gently pinching that person's cheek, like a little love tap."

"Well," he said with a grin, opening the door for her, snow falling outside, "so are you. We were invited to their home a week ago before all their family arrived, and we ate with her and Robert."

"They like us," Ali agreed. "And I love them because they are such generous people, trying every day to make this world a better place through their charities."

The snow fell silently around them as they stood on the screened porch. Ram locked the door and deposited the key into his pocket for the realtor back at Artemis. He saw the happiness on Ali's face as she stood watching the snowfall outside the protection of the porch roof. The house sat on a back road, it had been salted and the asphalt was gleaming in front of the home. Beyond that was a six-foot cyclone fence protecting the entire property. There was a maple tree in the front yard, carefully groomed bushes here and there, and a lot of rose bushes on the eastern side, which Ali delighted in. The lawn that surrounded the house was on three sides, now covered with a foot of new snow.

Ram could imagine this place in the summer. The Craftsman home was painted white with green trim, all conservative colors, but it melted into the nearby woodlands beyond the two acres of property. It was a good fit for them and his heart swelled with love for Ali. Soon, he would speak to her about it. Did she love him? She'd never said those words but he swore he saw it in her eyes.

"WHAT A NIGHT!" Ali said as Ram opened the

door to his condo for her. It was one a.m. and they'd just left the Culver's family Christmas party. Mazzie greeted them happily at the door and Ali leaned down, petting their dog. Ram carried two huge, brown bags filled with take-out containers of goodies packed by Dilara, just for them. There was food from Greece and Turkey, as well as Dilara's cooking, which was always spectacular and tasty.

"It was a lot of fun," he agreed.

Slipping inside, she closed the door after Ram entered. He went straight to the kitchen and Ali followed. How sexy he looked in his black chinos, and caramel-colored, wool blazer over a bright-red, long-sleeved tee that he'd worn for tonight's party.

She had enjoyed dressing up, wearing a velour, evergreen-colored set of trousers and matching blazer with a pink, ruffled cotton blouse beneath it. She went to the refrigerator and opened the door, knowing there were at least eight cardboard containers in those sacks that needed to be refrigerated.

"What a family they have!" Ali said, smiling as Ram gave her the first container. "I haven't done much traveling in that part of the world and have never met anyone from Turkey, except of course, Dilara and her children. But her three older brothers are wild. And each so different in personality from the others."

"Does it remind you of your own family?" he asked, passing on another container to her.

"It does. The warmth, the love, the laughter, and affection they have for each other is contagious." She sighed. "I love being in that kind of family environment. Did you enjoy it, Ram?"

"Yes. It's beginning to grow on me," he teased, smiling over at her. "You were the most beautiful woman there tonight. Did you know that, Aliyana?"

She felt heat color her cheeks as she continued to pack the food into the fridge. "Thank you, but I think you're a tad biased, Torres, don't you?"

"Nope," he said, folding up both sacks, and putting them away in another cabinet for use later. After Ali closed the door to the refrigerator, he slid his hand beneath her elbow, guiding her toward the living room. "There's something I need to give you."

Her brows rose. "But we have Christmas gifts under your tree," she said, pointing to a six-foot Scotch pine glittering with tree lights in the corner of the room.

"I know," he murmured patiently.

Ali felt a tension running through Ram, but didn't know why. They'd just had a wonderful meal with the Culver's extended family at their huge U-shaped dining room table. She'd covertly watched Ram relax—truly relax—among the little

United Nations of people he'd never met until tonight. Somewhere inside him, he yearned for that same kind of affectionate warmth with a family. *His own family.*

Ali yearned to give Ram that. He deserved a real, loving environment. And seeing him open up, begin to laugh, and take part socially with that family, meant so much to her. Beneath his fear he yearned for such a way of life that would feed his heart and soul, not try to destroy him as his own parents had almost done.

She tossed him a warm look as he sat down on the couch. Ram liked corners and he situated his large body against one end of the sofa, drawing her down beside him. Their thighs met one another and she gave him an expectant look. "What surprise do you have in store for me, Torres?" She watched him dig into his left, coat pocket.

"Well," he began, pulling out a dark-blue box and holding it out toward her, "I was trying to time when I'd do this. This is more than a Christmas gift, Aliyana." He took her hand, placing it in her palm. "This is something I've dreamed of doing for a long time."

The small, blue velvet box sat in her palm. "What have you done?" she whispered, assuming it was a ring box. But maybe she was wrong. Maybe he had bought her a pair of very expensive earrings? Ram knew she had a collection of small gold and pearl earrings that she loved to wear, but had rarely gotten to when she'd been a sniper. Now, working in an office every day, she'd worn them until she'd lost one of them. Perhaps Ram had replaced it?

"Something I hope you'll like, *mi tesoro.*"

Every time he called her "my treasure," her heart flew open with love for this man. It was becoming tougher not to whisper those words to him. Nervously, she sat the box down on her lap, fingers delicately pulling open the top of it.

Ali gasped. Her gaze flew to Ram and she saw the worry in his eyes. "Oh," she managed in a hoarse voice, "Ram . . ."

"Do you like them?" he asked hesitantly.

She gazed down at a yellow-diamond engagement ring paired with a gold wedding band. The band was a quarter of an inch wide and was burnished with leaves and flowers. Tears filled her eyes as she caressed the rings. "H-how did you know, Ram? How?" Ali lifted her chin, staring at him, her heart throbbing with so much love for this thoughtful man. "You want to marry me? Really? Not just live together?"

Ram swallowed against a constricting throat. He took her hands in his, holding her glimmering eyes wide with shock and happiness. "Of course I want to marry you, Aliyana. I love you. I've loved you for so long without realizing it, but it really hit me on that mission to rescue Cara and those other women. That's when I knew I loved you. It was damned hard for me to hide it from you. We were on a life-and-death mission and it was not the right place to explore how I felt about you romantically."

Nodding, she whispered, "I felt the same way about you, Ram. Seeing you again, and being with you on that op, I realized I loved you. I just didn't know what to do with it. I knew you were carrying a lot of dark secrets from your past and I felt walled out, but I also felt you trying to let me in, little by little, during that mission. And by the time you stayed with us after Cara was rescued, I really got to see more of the real you—the real Ram Torres."

"And even then, you didn't know about my past."

"No, but I saw enough in Tucson to realize there was hope that at some point I might approach you about a relationship, because I wanted one with you," she admitted, giving him a tender look. "I just didn't know how to go about it. We didn't have the privacy there to honestly talk to one another. Cara was our focus, as it should have been."

"Yes, you're right." Ram eased the engagement ring from the setting, placed the box aside, and turned her left hand over. "Will you marry me, Aliyana Montero? Be my wife, my best friend, my woman, the mother of any children we might have in the future?" His eyes bore into hers, his voice low and filled with a tremulous emotion she'd never heard before. "I love you. I've loved you from afar for so long. I will love you forever going forward. I want no other woman at my side except you. Will you marry me, *mi tesoro*?"

Tears streamed down her cheeks. Ali eased her finger through the engagement ring he held. "Y-yes, yes to everything you've just said. I'm more than ready to marry you, Ram. You are a part of my heart, my soul. You always have been and always will be . . . "

The ring fit perfectly, the golden facets glimmering and shifting. Now, finally, Ali realized just how deeply Ram loved her as she saw his relief when she agreed to marry him. She understood that even though some of their generation chose to just live together and not marry, it was important to Ram that they did. He would want any children they had to have their name, their foundation, and their love. Already, Ram was protective of her, and of their future children. Her heart flooded with joy. So much had been taken from him, but he was strong enough, and had the integrity to do the right thing for the right reasons for their future together. And Ali agreed fully with his needs because she loved him and wanted their children to have that parental umbrella of protection, too.

"Fits pretty well, doesn't it?" he asked, moving her hand, the facets flashing, a pleased look coming to his expression.

"It's perfect. I don't know how you did it."

He gave her a sly look. "Well, to tell you the truth, I called Mary and asked her to check the jewelry case in your room. I asked her to go look at one of the rings in it, get its size, and let me know."

"You're such a fox, Torres," she laughed. "Did Mama ask you why you wanted to know?"

"Yes, she did. I told her I wanted to marry you."

"Did she whoop, yell, and shout to the heavens?"

He chuckled, holding her hand in his. "No, she cried. I made her promise to say nothing to anyone until I could ask you. I was afraid you'd say no. I didn't tell your mother that, but it had to be a secret."

"I think," Ali whispered, leaning her cheek against his shoulder, "that you were afraid I'd say no because you heard the word through the actions of your own parents."

"In part, yes, but I knew you loved me. I saw it when we made love to each other, Aliyana. I saw it in so many large and small ways when we were at your parents' home. I saw it here when we agreed to live together. So many times, especially when loving you, I wanted to tell you that I loved you. But I was afraid of rejection, afraid of losing you when I'd just found you again. But I had to take a chance, anyway."

Nodding, Ali whispered, "You weren't the only one who was scared, Ram. Funny, I thought those same words, about taking a chance to reach out to you, too. At first, I was afraid to bring it up for the same reasons. So you see, we are similar in that way. I didn't want lose you, either. I didn't want to scare you off by saying I loved you because some men run at the word."

"I would never run from you," he rasped. "I will always run toward you." Releasing her hand, he slid his arm around her shoulders, drawing her gently against him. "I think we should go to bed now. I don't know that we'll get much sleep," he said, giving her a squeeze. "Then, tomorrow after breakfast, let's call Mary and Diego and tell them the good news? I'm sure Cara and Tyler will want to know, too."

"Wonderful, because it's Christmas Eve tomorrow," Ali said, nuzzling her cheek against his shoulder. "Mama and Papa will be so happy for us, Ram. For so long, they've wanted us girls to marry, to have children . . . this is a beautiful Christmas gift for them."

"I thought it might be. Do you have any idea when you might like to get married?" He searched her misty eyes, now gazing at him with such joy.

"I don't know . . . what about you?"

"Why don't we get married in Tucson? We can be close to your parents and Cara, maybe next March or April? What do you think?"

"Sounds perfect. Mama would hate to be left out of all the celebrations and by going there to marry, it will make them so happy." She saw a pleased look come to his eyes.

"I'm sure half of Artemis will want to be invited."

She laughed. "I'll talk to Alexa. She's the social butterfly here at Artemis. She'll help me with invitations and such."

"And you can work with Mary on the flowers from her garden for your bouquet."

"She'll love doing that," Ali whispered, suddenly emotional. She placed her hand on his chest, drowning in the love shining in his eyes for her alone. "And then, Ram, you will have a real family. No one deserves that more than you."

"I know, and whenever I think of that, Aliyana, I don't know if I can handle all that happiness. It's almost too much."

She patted his chest. "Get ready to be happier than you've ever been, Ram Torres. You're stuck with me now, giving you more love than you've ever dreamed of, and it will be multiplied by each of our children."

She saw his eyes fill with such emotion she thought he might burst into tears. Instead, he swept her into his arms, crushing her against him, holding her so tightly it squeezed the air out of her lungs.

Closing her eyes, she pressed a kiss to his chest. "*Te quiero con todo mi alma.* I love you with all of my soul . . . "

THE BEGINNING...

Don't miss Lindsay McKenna's
next DELOS series novella,
The Hidden Heart
Available wherever you buy
eBooks and paperbacks!

Turn the page for a sneak peek *The Hidden Heart*

Excerpt from

The Hidden Heart
by Lindsay McKenna

December 1

"**G**RAB HER!"

"Oh, no!" Cara Montero groaned as she watched one of Emilio Azarola's drug soldiers grab one of her fellow prisoners, blonde, attractive Inga in the large outdoor cage.

She watched mutely, still unable to believe she was actually living this nightmare. Two weeks ago, three drug dealers who had been driving around looking for women to kidnap to be sold as sex slaves overseas had dragged her off the streets of Tucson.

The day had been warm, bright and sunny, and women were out in numbers enjoying the fine weather and the local shops and bistros. No one expected to be snatched in broad daylight from the streets of a major city.

And then the men had spotted Cara, innocently walking down the street just blocks from her home. They screeched to a halt, grabbed her off the sidewalk and pushed her into the van. Stunned, unable to fathom what was happening, she had been wrestled to the floor by two masked men, held down, and injected with a drug that rendered her unconscious.

Then, she had been driven to a two-story villa deep in the mountains of Sonora, Mexico. Cara still didn't know where she was except for fragments of conversation she'd heard from the soldiers who spoke Spanish. She knew the men reported to a drug dealer named Emilio Azarola, but that was all. The three German tourists spoke a little English, enough that they could talk stiltedly between themselves.

She knew her gentle, loving parents, Mary and Diego Montero, must be frantic not knowing what had happened to their daughter and every day Cara prayed that someone would rescue her. The day after her abduction, three captured German tourists had joined her in her cell, and the four women had bonded in desperation, despite their language barrier.

Now, Inga screamed as one of the men grabbed her by the arm, dragging her toward the tall, rusty iron door, now open, where two more armed soldiers stood. She tried resisting, but the more she struggled, the more the men laughed. Finally, one of them cursed her in Spanish and slapped her hard, knocking her to the ground. She lay there, crumpled, as the other women gasped and shrank back, knowing what was coming next.

Cara pressed her hand across her mouth to stop from screaming, and watched as the woman was jerked upward, shakily standing barefoot before her gloating captors. The men had taken the women's shoes away so they couldn't escape. But where could they go? Deep mountain forest surrounded the area for as far as she could see. Dios, she wished she knew how close they were to the U.S. border!

The Books of Delos

Title: **Last Chance** (Prologue)
Publish Date: July 15, 2015
Learn more at:
delos.lindsaymckenna.com/last-chance

Title: **Nowhere to Hide**
Publish Date: October 13, 2015
Learn more at:
delos.lindsaymckenna.com/nowhere-to-hide

Title: **Tangled Pursuit**
Publish Date: November 11, 2015
Learn more at:
delos.lindsaymckenna.com/tangled-pursuit

Title: **Forged in Fire**
Publish Date: December 3, 2015
Learn more at:
delos.lindsaymckenna.com/forged-in-fire

Title: ***Broken Dreams***
Publish Date: January 2, 2016
Learn more at:
delos.lindsaymckenna.com/broken-dreams

Title: ***Blind Sided***
Publish Date: June 5, 2016
Learn more at:
delos.lindsaymckenna.com/blind-sided

Title: ***Secret Dream***
Publish Date: July 25, 2016
Learn more at:
delos.lindsaymckenna.com/secret-dream

Title: ***Hold On***
Publish Date: August 3, 2016
Learn more at:
delos.lindsaymckenna.com/hold-on

Title: ***Hold Me***
Publish Date: August 11, 2016
Learn more at
delos.lindsaymckenna.com/hold-me

Title: ***Unbound Pursuit***
Publish Date: September 29, 2016
Learn more at:
delos.lindsaymckenna.com/unbound-pursuit

Title: ***Secrets***
Publish Date: November 21, 2016
Learn more at:
delos.lindsaymckenna.com/secrets

Title: ***Snowflake's Gift***
Publish Date: February 4, 2017
Learn more at:
delos.lindsaymckenna.com/snowflakes-gift

Title: *Never Enough*
Publish Date: March 1, 2017
Learn more at:
delos.lindsaymckenna.com/never-enough

Title: *Dream of Me*
Publish Date: May 23, 2017
Learn more at:
delos.lindsaymckenna.com/dream-of-me

Title: *Trapped*
Publish Date: July 17, 2017
Learn more at:
delos.lindsaymckenna.com/trapped

Everything Delos!

Newsletter

Please visit my newsletter website at newsletter. lindsaymckenna.com. The newsletter will have exclusive information about my books, publishing schedule, giveaways, exclusive cover peeks, and more.

Delos Series Website

Be sure to drop by my website dedicated to the Delos Series at delos.lindsaymckenna.com. There will be new articles on characters, my publishing schedule, and information about each book written by Lindsay.